ALISTAIR MOORE

Flap Trap and Other Stories

Copyright © 2022 by Alistair Moore

All rights reserved. No part of this publication may be reproduced, stored or transmitted in any form or by any means, electronic, mechanical, photocopying, recording, scanning, or otherwise without written permission from the publisher. It is illegal to copy this book, post it to a website, or distribute it by any other means without permission.

Alistair Moore asserts the moral right to be identified as the author of this work.

This book is entirely a work of fiction. The names, characters and incidents portrayed in it are the work of the author's imagination. Any resemblance to actual persons, living or dead, events or localities is entirely coincidental.

Cover design by Alistair Moore

First edition

This book was professionally typeset on Reedsy. Find out more at reedsy.com

Contents

Preface	iv
Save the Future	1
Kickoff	16
LM039	19
The Box	44
A Better Place	52
Wires	76
Flap Trap	81
Zaiko's Game	114
About the Author	132
Also by Alistair Moore	133

Preface

These stories span a period of about 12 years. One of the earliest is *Kickoff*, a very short flash fiction style story about a protest spilling over into violence, which was adapted into a short film directed by my friend Zoran Trajkovic. The film did well, screening at many film festivals including Raindance in London and Berlin, Sundance (coming in the top 5 in the London Sundance Short Film Competition), the Brooklyn Shorts Film Festival in New York City, the Zero Film Festival in Los Angeles and not least, winning a prize – the UK Film Festival's Best British Short Award 2013. It stars Steven Waddington (*Sleepy Hollow, The Sweeney, Last of the Mohicans*) in the lead role. It can be found on YouTube and Vimeo as well as my website alistairmoore.com.

The eight stories vary a lot in length, style and tone, from the dark humour and surrealism of *LM039*, in which a narcissistic researcher tries to get a lab monkey to speak, to the satire of *Save the Future*, in which a spiritual guru clashes very publicly with a scientist. *The Box* is a memoir-like account of a First World War veteran reflecting on his life in his final years.

One recurring theme is the hubris of puffed-up authority figures and the perils of trusting blindly in them - something that has become unintentionally relevant over the past two years, with the world convulsed by the coronavirus pandemic.

I am also the author of *The Release* (Candy Jar Books 2018) a revenge-themed crime thriller with a literary feel. It is available from Amazon both in Kindle and Print, as well as from all good bookshops.

Save the Future

The crowd hushed as Jacob Fotzer, multi-millionaire tech entrepreneur and chair for the evening, stepped up to the podium. A small man, he was unmistakably middle-aged but dressed like a teenager in skinny black jeans and white trainers. His beard reached all the way down to the neckline of his t-shirt, which bore the event's name: Save the Future. He twiddled his hoop earring, cleared his throat and addressed the audience in a California twang.

"The theme of tonight's event, long in the making, is nothing less than humanity's greatest challenge; our survival as a species. We held the largest ever non-political public poll to pick two candidates to discuss the greatest dangers of our time. These threats to humanity were also voted on by you, the people. Top of the list, with more combined votes than all other topics, is climate change."

Affirmative murmurs hummed round the auditorium.

"The rest of the list, by descending order of popularity. War." Fotzer paused again for dramatic effect, but the hum was quieter this time. "Famine. Toxins in our food and water. Deadly pandemics. Environmental pollution." He stroked his beard and adjusted the microphone. "Systemic racism. Structural sexism. Unequal distribution of wealth," he said with relish, for he felt these should have been top of the list. Some groans arose, for this big event had captured the interest of those of all political persuasions.

"Virtually all these problems were created by…" Fotzer stopped again and swiveled to survey the great hall from left to right, near and far, lower and upper levels. "Us. We are responsible. So our two guests, chosen as the greatest thinkers of our generation, will ponder two questions tonight. Firstly, what the hell is wrong with us? Secondly, how do we save the future for those who will follow?"

The lights dimmed, and a dramatic orchestral score sounded from the network of speakers mounted high across the vaulted ceilings.

"In the blue corner, representing science, numbers and logic, originally hailing from Great Britain, we have the world's most eminent data scientist."

Stage beams came on to Fotzer's right, shrouding a seated silhouette in a halo of light. The host now spoke in a dramatic, lowered tone as if voicing a film trailer.

"His mother endured a thirty-six hour labour due to the unusual size of his head, leading doctors to verify that his brain was thirty-five percent larger than that of an average male newborn. By six months, he had gained the vocabulary of a five year-old. By age nine, he was fluent in five languages. Although he excelled with distinctions in every subject, he had a special affinity for mathematics and, as a fellow at Oxford University in England, was taken under the tutelage of the great maths professor Matthew Barbage. Barbage's mentorship set him on a path to applying his abilities to solve some of the greatest questions of our time. He now runs several leading AI projects at Stanford and MIT. His achievements are too numerous to reel off here, but many of the awards he has received relate to his work using artificial intelligence to dramatically improve health outcomes for millions. It is his firm belief that humanity's salvation lies in technology. It is my great honour and pleasure to introduce to you – Doctor Wendell Chive."

The lights went up stage right, illuminating the guest. Loud cheers and whoops arose across the auditorium. A hint of a smile showed on Chive's thin lips. He rolled his great head back, closed his eyes for the duration of the applause and then as it died down, gave a small, gracious nod.

"In the red corner, standing for spiritualism, an individual who has been on an incredible journey, from the Himalayas, across Europe and South America, and to our great pleasure, with us tonight here in Palo Alto."

Now sounds of skin drums and twisting sitar chords echoed across the great hall. The low beam to Fotzer's left threw up a fan of light behind the second guest. The silhouetted figure appeared tall, even though seated.

"The youngest of eight siblings, he was born into a family of yak farmers in the mountains of India. He grew up with little, but displayed an astounding connection with nature, developing the ability to speak with animals aged three. One morning, his parents awoke to find the farm deserted and all the beasts gone. When the child confessed he had told the yaks to pursue their freedom, his enraged father abandoned him in a mountain cave. He was discovered there days later by a wandering fakir who adopted him. The fakir recognised something special in the boy, and became his spiritual mentor as well as his guardian. Within just a few years, he became one of the best-known spiritual teachers in the East. While his fame spread to the Western world, he put his wealth to use building new irrigation systems, schools and hospitals for millions across India, Bhutan and Nepal. He believes that spirituality can save us. We are honoured to welcome, here, tonight at Save the Future, Swami Langsam."

The Swami was illuminated for all to see, revealing his dark-lidded eyes closed as Chive's had been. His long, glossy black hair hung down over his orange robes. His skin, a rich golden brown, shone brightly in the iridescence of the footlights. The clapping and cheering seemed to go on for even longer than his predecessor's. "We love you!" cried a man's voice near the front. The Swami's eyes flicked open and he cast a benevolent smile down toward the ardent devotee.

Glowing with satisfaction at his introductions, which he felt had gone splendidly, Fotzer turned to address the audience. "Now we know Doctor Chive also has many fans, especially female ones. We have a lot of 'Chivettes' out there, am I right?"

Squeals erupted from all quarters.

"We know you're here, because we had several mass bookings from 'The Sapiosexual Society', which was offering a discount on tonight's event. Similarly, tens of thousands identifying themselves as followers of Swami Langsam overwhelmed our booking systems. In order to give the general public a fair chance at securing places tonight, we limited places for both groups to fifty percent of the venue's capacity. Which means there's still a hell of a lot of you!"

Shouts, cheers and whoops filled the air.

"So we've got a lively audience. Let's hope for an equally lively yet fruitful discussion tonight. You could say… our future depends on it."

Fotzer variously turned to face the men either side of him.

"Swami Langsam, perhaps you can kick off the open discussion with your thoughts on the first question. Where did we go wrong?"

The Swami stared into the distance for so long it appeared he hadn't heard the question. Murmurs arose from the crowd.

"We lost our way long ago," he said finally in a thick Indian accent. "We are selfish and self-obsessed, driven only by material gain and external validation. We cannot prevail while we remain absorbed by petty quarrels, desire for fame and other manifestations of the ego. The seeds have been sown, and now they are bearing fruit." Once again he was silent. Fotzer waited and then finally drew breath to speak. "And the fruit is rotten," the Swami continued with vehemence, then closed his eyes and nodded, indicating he'd concluded his thoughts.

"Do you agree, Doctor Chive?" said Fotzer.

"Not entirely," replied the Doctor in a transatlantic drawl. "The problem is we have become vain and greedy. We spend our time manufacturing conflicts instead of helping others. We are prioritising the self over the common good of humanity."

The Swami chuckled aloud, shaking his head.

"Listening to you both, it does sound as if you agree," said Fotzer. "That's a good start, right?" he said to the audience with a smile.

"But if I may," continued Chive, "I object to this idea that things have only gotten worse. Never mind developments over the last hundred years. If we simply look at the last ten years, we've seen an unheard of level of innovation and progress. We're developing the means to improve quality of life not marginally, but exponentially."

"And how are you measuring such things?" said the Swami. "By whose yardstick do you define this exponential improvement? You think you can sum up all of human experience like this?"

"I'm unsure whether the esteemed Swami is being intentionally facetious," said Chive. "But there are very concrete, tangible metrics in common use. If I may call upon my colleague to demonstrate," Chive said to Fotzer. "Of course," replied the host, and in a clearly pre-planned sequence, a bespectacled Asian man climbed up onstage. He nodded shyly towards the audience and set about connecting a tablet device to the large screen above the podium.

"May I introduce one of the world's finest mathematicians, a renowned statistician and my good friend, Professor Kim Kong," said Chive. The screen lit up with an array of graphs, mostly showing a series of blue lines snaking up ever more sharply rightwards.

"Even the most generalised quality of life indices use widely accepted parameters, measuring such things as life expectancy, rates of serious illness, self-reported happiness and many more," said Chive. All these metrics, which I repeat are universally recognised, show a dramatic uptrend in recent years."

Chive stopped for a moment, for the Swami was chuckling loudly. "Perhaps the Swami would like us to return to the dark ages. To prehistory, maybe? A Hobbesian world where simply by sitting here, we'd have both radically beaten the odds to remain alive?"

"This is nothing new," said the Swami, addressing the audience. "The arrogance of the Western approach. Your so-called logic is the solution to everything. I wish not to insult Mr Kong, who I know and hold in high esteem, but these charts, diagrams and numbers, are mere sophistry."

"The fact you don't understand this data does not qualify you to dismiss it," retorted Chive. "Indeed, it's the opposite. And incidentally, this is about far more than logic. We're beyond logic. We have advanced technologically in ways which are, dare I say it, outside your comprehension."

The Swami chuckled once more. Professor Kong shifted awkwardly, tablet in hand.

"In any case, all this data is available online, and in my recent publications," said Chive to the audience. "Thank you, Kim." The professor resumed his place in the front row.

"Humanity is not made of numbers," said the Swami.

"You're wrong," said Chive. "Everything we know derives from numbers. Our genetic code, our DNA, our chromosomes. The elements. Atomic and subatomic structures. The matter of the universe."

"Can that be possible?" chimed in the host. "That everything is just numbers?"

"It's not quite that simple," said Chive. "Numbers are the root of everything. But there is a better way to look at it, which I explain in my latest book. Everything – and I mean everything – can be grouped into one of two categories. Nodes and layers."

"Can you explain to us what that means?"

"By nodes I mean nodes, the existing definition. Self contained units, typically interconnected with other units in a network, grid or hierarchy."

"Are we nodes?" said Fotzer.

"Human beings are nodes. As are animals, insects,

all organisms."

"What about inanimate objects?"

"Also nodes, or node clusters. Built from atoms. Atoms are nodes."

"Nodes within nodes."

"Correct."

"And what is meant by your definition of layers?"

"Layers are states of being across networks. It's hard to fully explain in brief, but it applies to a great many things – colour, tone, temperature, emotional mood, age, just as a few examples. Layers often span node clusters, and are often nested within themselves, like nodes."

"What do you make of this theory?" said Fotzer to the guru, who was rolling his eyes.

"He's plagiarised Hindu beliefs. The Doctor has simply given new names to chakras and spiritual realms, and is now claiming these as his own ideas."

"So in a sense you do agree with the theory?" attempted Fotzer.

"Not only do we disagree," said the Swami, "but we're continuing an old debate, which his side has never satisfactorily addressed. His big data fails to explain the most fundamental questions of the soul. Forgive me, but the idiocy of categorising people as 'nodes'…"

"In your case, a defective node," said Chive.

"Aha! Insults now. And what of my devotees?"

"Them too," fired back Chive. Commotion grew across various sections of the audience, and shouts rang out across the great hall.

"Calm please," said Fotzer, and the noise died down only a little.

"Quite something to be called a plagiarist by a liar," said Chive.

"Oh?" said the Swami with a grin.

"Whatever your other abilities, your talent for comic fiction is unrivalled. Take that little introduction of yours. You sit here without a trace of shame claiming a childhood ability to speak with dumb animals. Perhaps you can demonstrate this skill to us?"

"I'm speaking with you, am I not?"

Roars erupted from the crowd and a plastic bottle bounced off Fotzer's podium. "Okay now," said the host in a stern yet slightly anxious voice. "No misbehaving. We promised a lively discussion and that's what we've got, but any attendees breaking the rules will be removed immediately.

"So our problem is obsession with material gain, as you put it earlier," said Chive. "Perhaps you can tell your devotees how your fleet of four Maseratis and three Rolls Royces, and your property empire worth twenty-five million dollars, plus the forty million you have in offshore accounts, is currently benefiting humanity?"

"How about we tell the audience your plagiarism goes beyond ripping off Hindu ideas," replied the Swami. "My sanyassins found out some very interesting things about you, oh yes."

"Uh, we do have a list of topics to move through," said Fotzer. "If we can…"

"That project you won all those awards for. The predictive algorithm that reduced illness rates in seven countries," said the Swami.

Chive sat stony and silent, his jaw muscles clenching.

"Wasn't your work at all, was it?"

Fotzer looked at Chive in apparent surprise, but still the Doctor said nothing.

"Ladies and gentlemen," said Swami Langsam, "the algorithm that made this man famous was written by none other than his assistant, Professor Kim Kong."

Gasps and shouts arose. Heads turned towards the empty seat where Professor Kong had, moments earlier, been sitting.

"But you took the credit," said Langsam. "And when he objected, you threatened to have the visa you'd arranged for him by forging documents cancelled. You said he'd be on the first plane back to Korea."

"Lies," said Chive shaking his head. "Absolute nonsense."

"Sue me then," said the Swami. "If I'm wrong, go

ahead and call your lawyer."

"Oh I will, don't worry," said the Doctor. The crowd had grown rowdy again. Fotzer stepped up to the microphone.

"If everyone can settle down a little, we'll move to the next phase of the discussion," he said. "As you've seen, we have two very differing approaches tonight. In addition to their immense achievements and respective influences across the world, both our guests have strong opinions to match. Which means not only those here tonight, but millions of others watching will now be wondering; what if these two great minds were to combine forces and work together towards solving humanity's problems?"

"You're not from the Himalayas, you cunt," said Chive.

"Er, gentlemen…" pleaded Fotzer as Chive stood up, a head taller than him.

"Fraud," shouted the Doctor over the host's head at the Swami, who had also risen to his feet.

"You're not even Indian. I had my people look into you. You're from England. You're an electrician from Neasden in North-West London. You got convicted for criminal negligence after a family house burned down. You fled the country and changed your identity. Scotland Yard are still looking for him," said Chive to the audience, who were now in uproar. Projectiles flew across the auditorium.

"And what are you going to do about it, melon-head?" said the Swami, his Indian accent replaced by something distinctly more British. Chive lunged and swung at the guru, clipping Fotzer's ear on the way. "Security, now," squealed Fotzer into his tie mic as he became entrapped in a tangle of flailing arms and orange robes. "Get out the way," shouted a voice from the front row. "Let 'em fight!" yelled another.

Burly men carrying radios pushed their way through the unruly crowds now filling the aisles. Fotzer finally extricated himself from the two grappling men, who promptly keeled over together and rolled around the stage. Several fistfights had broken out in the stalls. The host, somewhat dazed, looked down to see that his 'Save the Future' t-shirt was not only torn, but smeared with bronze stains. It was then he noticed the Swami's complexion now had two shades – his original brown skin tone on one side, and on a large swathe of the other side of his face, an increasingly more Caucasian shade.

By the time the PAPD officers arrived, the scene had all the hallmarks of a mass riot, despite the two main guests having now been separated. Men wrestled and traded punches, women fought with women, pulling hair, scratching and slapping. Several seats had been ripped from their fittings, and plastic cups and bottles littered the auditorium. Official footage of the evening was mysteriously lost due to technical issues, but the event was hailed in the media as a great success.

Kickoff

There's a strange calm before it all begins. You'd think it just builds up and up until it finally erupts, but right before it goes off, there's always a moment of quiet. It's like everyone's taking a deep breath and steeling themselves, maybe even praying. It's almost eerie. How do I know this? Well, this isn't my first one. I'm a veteran. I've been doing this for years. I was doing this before I was old enough to drive.

People often ask me what it feels like to be right in the middle of it. Exciting? Frightening? Well, I say, it's both. But what I feel more strongly than anything else is the solidarity. To my left, to my right, and behind me, my comrades stand tight, like bricks in a wall. It's a powerful feeling, a wonderful feeling. We're no idiots. We're organised this time. No man will be left behind.

Some people disapprove. They say we're thugs who simply crave violence. They accuse us of having no proper understanding of the political issues, the injustices, no comprehension of the real reasons behind and need for resistance. But truthfully, I don't give a damn what they think. It's no crime not to be political. I've never really wanted or needed to be. You can have views and opinions without being interested in parliament. That stuff bores the shit out of me.

We didn't want to get caught out like we were before, so we studied this time. We watched footage from riots all over the world. We really got some inspiration – take the French, for example. Now they really know how to have a riot. Like everything else, they've practically turned it into an art form. We English are too timid.

It's beginning to kick off now. The helicopters are lower, much closer, louder; I can actually feel the thumping of the rotor blades reverberating in my bones. They're watching everything from up there; got to be careful. Best not to show your face if you can help it. My heart, like the helicopters above, is pounding. I feel it in my throat.

Near my left flank, about twenty feet away, a riot van is edging through the crowd. There is a splat of red paint across the windshield and the steel grille covering it. Coins rain down onto the van… thunk, thunk, thunk. From somewhere comes a shoe. It bounces off the roof. A man with a patterned scarf round his face jumps up and repeatedly punches the passenger window with a gloved fist. The passenger doesn't react, the driver doesn't react. Those windows are tough. The van doesn't change its speed but simply ploughs onward like a slow, white armadillo. Now people are spitting on the windows.

Plastic bottles containing liquid are flying through the air. Turning around once more, I look at my companions' faces. Some look frightened, but most look like excited children. They are actually smiling. I am smiling too. The noise levels are building up now. The shrill whine of the megaphones battles with the noise from the choppers above and the chants from the crowd.

Then without explanation, the noise dies right back down again. Even the sound from the choppers is muted. For a few seconds, there is something close to silence.

"Here we go, boys," shouts one of our group. "It's on!"

Whoops and cheers surround me, elbows jostle. My feet are hardly touching the ground, but I am moving. We surge forward as one. Then my feet find the ground again. The moment we've been waiting for has arrived, at last. Snapping down my visor, I step forward and enter the fray.

LM039

Dr Kremble was in a bad mood. Things just seemed to keep going wrong, small things which ruined the bigger picture. He'd had his eye on Harriet for months, and now, after all his plans for her, she'd been taken.

Harriet, one of the last generation of lab monkeys given human names, had been perfect in every way. It was well-known that females were better communicators, but Harriet was especially intelligent, with a curiosity unblunted by age. But as luck would have it, after nearly a year of preparation, when everything was finally ready, she was poached by cosmetics.

Kremble had complained, he'd kicked up as much of a stink as he'd been able. His work was actually important. It could provide stunning new insights into the way the brain developed communication and language faculties. Textbooks might be rewritten. But instead, Harriet's ideal qualities were being utterly wasted on testing new brands of moisturiser.

Kremble fumed at the obscenity of it as he walked alongside the monkey enclosure.

There was nothing to be done about it, of course. The pharma companies had all the money, so they had all the power. Comparatively, Kremble's clout was non-existent. Since he'd secured funding the project was pretty much his baby, his alone to organise and run. Nobody else had taken much interest in it.

One of the monkeys he passed was pressed against the glass, palms flat, showing his teeth. Kremble stopped and looked at the name tag, which read LM039. They'd stopped using human names a decade ago, mainly because humanising them caused problems. More than once, lab workers had developed attachments to the monkeys. In one case it had resulted in a security breach as the compound had been opened up and the monkeys let loose around the building. On another occasion, an intern had surreptitiously filmed some of the experiments and released them to an animal rights organisation. The fallout had been disastrous.

Kremble looked at the sheet. LM039 was an eight year-old male. The doctor leaned forward. LM039's lips peeled back further, showing his gums. He extended a brown finger towards Kremble's face. The leathery digit tapped at the partition.

LM039 hadn't been assigned to any physical experiments, but he'd been used in separation and bonding studies. Two groups, one brought up from infancy by their mothers, the other separated and isolated, had been studied throughout childhood and adolescence, given identical tests and placed in identical situations. Most of those from Gamma, the separation group, had suffered severe emotional difficulties, finding it impossible to bond and communicate with other monkeys and living their lives in a state of depression and isolation. Some had self-harmed, and one had simply died at three years with no obvious cause.

LM039 was from Gamma. What was remarkable about him, however, was that unlike the others orphaned by his test group, he had turned out apparently normal, behaving exactly as a young adult monkey should. He integrated well with other monkeys. His temperament was described as sociable, amiable, co-operative, and restless.

LM039 hadn't been assigned to any projects since. Nobody had found a use for him yet. The conclusion from the separation and bonding study was that LM039 had been the only one from Gamma to thrive emotionally because he scored significantly above average in three areas: self-sufficiency, adaptation and communication. The doctor fixed upon this last word for some time.

Behind the lockable compartments, one of which

LM039 was staring at Kremble from right now, was a shared play area with straw bedding, a climbing frame, and a tyre hanging from a rope. For two hours each day the compartments were opened up and the monkeys allowed to mingle. It was also part of the breeding programme.

LM039 was a father to three healthy, happy infants, LM934, LM935 and LF394, who were lucky enough to be looked after by their mothers, LF150 and LF021. Kremble replaced LM039's info sheet and scratched his thick black eyebrows, as he did when deep in thought. LM039 scratched his head in turn, mimicking the doctor.

Within days it was done. The application was processed quickly, and LM039 was assigned to Wendrick Kremble, Bachelor, Master and Doctor of Linguistics, Semiotics and Neuroscience. After Kremble's signature and several countersignatures, LM039 was taken to theatre, sedated, and had the rear section of his cranium removed. This, however, was not to be an 'open-top' experiment – the type where monkeys were subjected to various tests with their skulls opened up, probes and electrodes embedding into their visible brains.

This was a much more sophisticated study, and one which was unlikely to work with the subject distracted by the knowledge that the top of his head was missing.

Kremble had first developed the idea when he learned of Nanoboosters, tiny chip implants designed to stimulate hard-to-reach areas with electrical currents. They held electrical charge for months and had been successfully used in treating muscle atrophy, erectile dysfunction and in one case, partial paralysis.

Of course, experiments into apes' understanding of human language and communication were nothing new. Chimps had been taught to recognise certain symbols and vocalisations. But nothing like this had been attempted before.

Wernicke's area, a part of the posterior cerebral hemisphere governing written and spoken language in humans, had an equivalent in most primates. Kremble's idea was a fairly simple one. To embed the Nanobooster nodes in the cerebral cortex, hyperstimulate Wernicke's area, and attempt to turboboost the monkey's language capabilities. No lifetime of schooling in human language was needed – this was specifically about the effect of the stimulation of that part of the brain, rather than the ability of primates to learn language and symbology over the long term. In any case, all monkeys in the compound were subjected to daily radio broadcasts, as a basic foundation for the numerous language studies they were often appropriated for.

Yes, Kremble had rivals, of course he did. But they

tended to be overcautious, excessively reliant on collaboration, as if scared to strike out by themselves; no originality. He didn't like associating with them.

At first he'd been surprised nobody seemed particularly thrilled by his idea, then offended, then finally pleased. It was better he was left to manage it himself. Who cared if they thought he was a crank. If there was a breakthrough, the credit would be entirely his. Furthermore, he could do without his every move being scrutinised and recorded by panels made up of his peers and various other meddlers and overseers. It was ideal.

When LM039 was finally out of theatre a week later, he seemed more or less the same monkey he'd been before, which was encouraging. Finally alone with his subject, Kremble could begin. The room he had chosen had all but the most essential fixtures and fittings removed so that the monkey could move around freely. The more natural things were, the better.

LM039 sat in a chair before a large, white desk, his head bandaged, eating peanuts from a paper bowl and watching Kremble as he set up the equipment; a video camera in the corner pointed at both of them, and a laptop computer, which was plugged in via the desk to the large, wall-mounted VDU. Attached to the laptop was a pair of speakers and modified keyboard, which he placed on the desk in front of

LM039. The keys were enlarged, and lit up and made a chiming sound when pressed.

Kremble tried to get LM039 to press the keys, but the monkey showed no interest. The doctor pressed them himself to demonstrate, the letters flashing large on the screen on the wall, singly and in sequence. LM039 picked his fur, scratched his gonads, spat peanuts across the room and even got up onto Kremble's shoulders, but he would not press the keys on the special, modified keyboard.

This went on for several days, and Kremble began to suspect LM039 was just being bloody-minded. They should have put it on the monkey's info sheet. Sociable, amiable, co-operative, restless, bloody-minded. Still, he was patient. He had to be. He was a scientist, not a musician or an athlete. These things took time.

On the fourth day, there was a breakthrough. It happened, as things often did, at the moment Kremble finally felt at the end of his rope with it all. LM039, amongst other things, had taken to masturbating at him. He'd climb out of the chair onto the desk, avoiding the keyboard, and sit with his furred thighs spread, flicking his thin, scarlet phallus, looking at Kremble with bared teeth.

"Just stop it!" shouted the doctor. "Will you stop doing that!"

LM039 stopped, his lips curled back around his

teeth, and then he stood up, shuffled sideways, and prodded at the keyboard by his feet. The speakers chimed and a large K flashed up on the VDU.

Kremble's heart thumped in excitement. Although part of him knew it was ridiculous to get excited simply at the fact he'd pressed a key – after all, monkeys played with anything in sight, so it was stranger that he hadn't for so long – he couldn't help but wonder if there was some significance in the K. Was he saying OK? OK, I'll stop masturbating at you? After all, he'd done as asked. For nearly two hours Kremble tried to get him to push keys again, but LM039 showed no interest. He yawned, stretched, did cartwheels and slept.

"Since breakthrough at 3.42pm, nothing," said Kremble into a hand-held voice recorder. "Repeated attempts to replicate so far unsuccessful."

No progress was made for the next few days. It seemed LM039 was happy to mess with every piece of equipment except the part Kremble wanted him to. He picked up the laptop, pushed the speakers onto the floor, tugged at the screen on the wall, succeeded twice in toppling the camera and tripod, and made numerous attempts to grab the voice recorder from the doctor's hands.

Wendrick Kremble was beginning to lose sleep. He was plagued by dreams of failure, of looming walls which he would scale, only to fall off as he neared the top. Colleagues began asking if he was well, one even congratulating him on his ongoing contribution to Doctor Harpreet Singh's new sleep deprivation project, about which he knew absolutely nothing. He decided to give it one more day, then end the experiment. The monkey could be reused. The booster chips wouldn't need to be removed as they'd lose their power after a couple of months and simply become dormant.

Kremble began early in the morning, at dawn. If this was to be the final shot, he'd have to make the most of it. As usual, one of the keepers who managed the animal compounds brought LM039 to the testing room. The monkey took his usual place behind the desk while the doctor checked the equipment. As Kremble moved around in front of the tripod to make sure there were no simian fingerprints smudging the camera's lens, he felt something hit the back of his neck with a stinging slap. He span around to see LM039 standing on the chair with his hairy arms outstretched. Kremble reached around to his nape and felt something soft and warm. The smell hit his nostrils about the same time he saw the faeces on his palm. He roared out loud. LM039 responded by hopping onto the table and baring his teeth, his curled lips quivering and wet.

"Kraaaa!" said LM039.

A knock came at the door. "Are you okay in there? What's going on?"

"It's okay," shouted Kremble. "I dropped something. There's no problem."

The doctor slowly picked up the recorder with his unsoiled hand, keeping his eyes on the subject.

"Subject throwing his excreta. Increase in aggression."

As he cleaned his hand and the back of his neck with wet wipes, he heard several chimes in succession. He span around.

SORRY, read the VDU.

LM039 was still sitting on the desk, his hands poised over the keyboard. Kremble checked the video camera. It was all working, the little red recording light glowing. Everything was recorded; the computer program captured every keystroke. He wondered if he was hallucinating. He'd been shocked at his own reflection that morning. His eyes seemed to be turning into large, dark cavities.

"You... you're sorry?"

LM039 looked at Kremble for a while, then at the keyboard beneath him. He extended a finger and tapped three areas on the large, doormat-sized keyboard.

YES, chimed the large letters on the screen.

Kremble realised he was standing between the video camera and LM039, and moved aside. LM039 was looking at the doctor in what was considered in monkeys to be a friendly manner; his head inclined to one side, lips covering his teeth.

"Then why did you do it?" said Kremble, his voice quivering.

LM039 leaned forward and hit the keys again.

HUNGRY, read the VDU.

Kremble turned back to look at LM039, then the VDU, then at the video camera in the corner, then back at LM039.

"I'll be right back," said Kremble. He edged backwards toward the door, keeping his eyes on the monkey. As he fumbled for the handle, LM039 began to scratch between his legs, shaking his head vigorously from side to side.

Kremble ran all the way to the animal compound, his mind aflame. He had to repeat himself several times before the keeper understood him.

"Nuts," said Kremble. "Give me nuts, a kilo of nuts. Seeds, bananas, everything you feed the monkeys. Hurry!"

When he returned clutching paper bags in each hand, LM039 was asleep.

"Here," said Kremble, placing the opened bags on the desk. LM039 woke up, bared his teeth at the doctor, lifted a handful of nuts to his mouth, then pushed the bags aside. The next few hours yielded nothing. It seemed LM039 wanted nothing more than to rest. When the keeper came to take the monkey back to the compound, the doctor was extremely nervous about letting him go.

"Give him anything he wants," he said, his fingers clenching the keeper's sleeve. "Make sure he's safe," added Kremble as the keeper finally disengaged himself from the doctor's grip. "I need him back here first thing. Eight in the morning, on the dot. No later, you hear me?"

Kremble decided to spend the night in the lab, availing himself of one of the fold-up beds kept for those who had to pull all-nighters. He locked himself into the room and spent hours going over the footage. Although all three keystroke sequences that day had been recorded, time-stamped and logged by the computer's software, he'd ruined the video of LM039 typing SORRY and YES. What he did have was an excellent close-up of his own facial expression as the wad of dung struck the back of his neck, and crucially, clear footage of LM039 keying in the word HUNGRY. He watched it about twenty-five times before deciding he should get some sleep. Sleep, however, was a long time in coming. Scenarios raced through his feverish mind, him on a podium before a large screen, his audience filled with men and women of immense learning and influence. He wondered what he should wear for television; casual clothing, a suit, finally deciding on his white lab coat. As the first birds of dawn chirped outside, Kremble finally drifted away.

He was woken no more than three hours later by the keeper knocking. Kremble struggled to open his eyes as he opened the door. The keeper released LM039's hand, and the monkey bounded into the test room, in evident good spirits.

Kremble was exhausted, but he'd at least had the foresight to prime the equipment before going to bed. As he pulled on his lab coat he resolved to be calm. It was clear neither coercion or anger would yield results. Furthermore if he did not control himself, excitement and anxiety would ruin his focus. The night before he had laid out mounds of nuts, seeds, berries and other assorted fruit on the desk. LM039 jumped up and shoveled the treats into his mouth. With the subject occupied, Kremble slipped out of the room, careful to lock it behind him.

Minutes later he returned with a second, identical video camera and tripod. As LM039 tore through the piles of provisions, Kremble set up the second camera in the other corner. With both cameras running and the software fired up, he buttoned up his lab coat, stroked his chin and felt the roughness of three days of stubble, something he'd not known since he was a student. He wished he'd remembered to shave, but there was no more time to be lost.

He stood before camera one and cleared his throat. "Day eight of the simian neuro-linguistic enhancement project." He cleared his throat again. "Day eight of the primate neurolingual nanoboost project." He could edit everything later. "This has never been attempted before. Already, the results have been beyond spectacular. I intend to document history. Until now, everything we have believed…" he stopped again. "The very foundation of the way we…" he stopped again, and scratched his thick eyebrows. "I, Doctor Wendrick Stapleton Kremble, conceived and designed this project, and am primary and sole researcher. Behind me is LM039, an eight year-old male cynomolgus macaque born into group Gamma as part of the Hoyst-Birdsley bonding and separation programme. It is my belief….owwww!"

Kremble stepped aside to show camera one LM039, who was flicking peanuts at him from a cupped hand.

"I present the subject."

Kremble was very careful not to show anger. He would not risk any more face-offs. Macaques often carried Simian Herpes, which had caused death in humans. There was wide scepticism about the claims that all monkeys in the compound were certified disease-free. Kremble cautiously lobbed peanuts back at LM039, which seemed to settle him down, and he in turn felt more relaxed. Perhaps it would take days, weeks. It didn't matter now. The breakthrough had been made. He just needed the subject to stay alive and the Nanoboosters to keep working.

If worst came to worst, he still had the HUNGRY footage. You could clearly see the monkey hitting the enlarged keys in sequence. It would be held up to intense scrutiny, of course. They'd say the footage was faked, or if they acknowledged it was real, they'd say he'd literally lucked out with the Infinite Monkey Theorem, even though the chances were one in twenty-six to the power of six – a 0.0000000032 per cent probability. Academic science was not the collaborative utopia it made itself out to be. It was competitive, dishonest and cut-throat, and there was no doubt Kremble would be slandered, plagiarised and stabbed in the back over this. If they couldn't get a slice of his glory, they'd do their best to sabotage it.

But it would all be worth it. Finally, having tired of eating and throwing food, LM039 positioned himself in front of the keyboard. Kremble got to his feet, moved out of view of the cameras, and waited. Now using two hands, LM039 tapped out a sequence;

YBSUBEP

The doctor strained to think. Another language? He'd have to check it, cross-reference it with every vocabulary known to man. Perhaps it was something he'd heard on the radio. The monkey hit the keys again.

OOJFHSJU

said the screen, and again

IOUFHW

He seemed to be hitting them indiscriminately now, not looking at what he was doing.

"I know you can do this. Come on!"

The doctor felt the agitation rise up within him. No worthy success, he told himself, came easily. And now the subject had begun using both hands to hit the keys, which had to be significant. LM039 shook his wrists and began to type again.

VOICE, read the VDU. LM039 blinked and snorted at Kremble, who was breathing heavily. The doctor looked into camera two and spoke quietly.

"Once again, this is the evidence of test subject LM039, a monkey, communicating with human language."

LM039 was typing again.

GIVE ME A VOICE, said the VDU.

"A voice?" said the doctor. "What do you mean?"

LM039 opened his mouth wide and made a noise like static crackle, then began to pick at the fur on his belly.

Then he remembered the software had a text-to-speech module. To use it hadn't even occurred to him; it wasn't something he'd prepared for. He opened up the laptop on the desk and activated speech as LM039 poked him repeatedly in the side. He stood back.

LM039 snorted and then began to type, using two digits on each hand to strike the large keys.

ARSEFACE, said an Americanised robotic, monotone voice.

Kremble fumbled for the voice recorder, then realised he didn't need it.

"Subject's vocabulary includes profanities," he said, looking towards camera two.

LM039 again began hitting keys apparently at random, and the robot voice tried to make a word from them.

NKXBSHF, it said.

"Come on," breathed Kremble. "Keep going."

CHANGE VOICE, droned the speech module as LM039 tapped away, much more quickly now.

Kremble clicked around the interface looking for options. The speaking voice was set to a default named neutral. There was a range of options available including gender and accent, with scores of nationalities and even regions available for each. There were sliders for speech characteristics such as pitch, range, expressiveness and intonation, as well as a range of preset, ready-calibrated options. He went for Male Southern English Baritone.

"Try that," said Kremble.

TRY. YES, said a deep and pleasing voice as the subject hammered out the words.

"Wonderful," said Kremble. "Wonderful."

The monkey tapped again.

POXY COCK.

"As yet, it's impossible to say exactly why the subject is focusing on this kind of language," said Kremble into camera two, trying himself to sound as baritone as possible. "It can only have been learned from the radio broadcasts played to the benched test monkeys. But what is truly incredible here is the sheer speed of this accelerated, boosted learning. LM039 has not only learned to use human language in a matter of days, but his input skills are improving at an astonishing rate."

TOSS. ARSE. TOSSARSE.

said the baritone over Kremble. He turned around. The monkey was tapping maniacally.

DICKBREATH.

The doctor approached to get a closer look at the subject's movements.

"Kraaaaaaaaaaaaaaaa!" said LM039, standing up straight with his arms in the air.

"Okay, okay," said Kremble, backing off. "Take it easy."

LM039 continued to vocalise as he trampled the

keyboard underfoot, so that the baritone reading of single letters

W, J, K, R, R, R

was blended with the noises emitting from LM039's mouth.

"You've had enough?" said Kremble, trying to sound soothing. "We can stop, it's fine."

LM039 jumped off the desk onto the floor in one movement and began to run up the wall and somersault backwards repeatedly.

"I think this concludes today's studies," said Kremble, feeling proud his patience was working to his advantage. He was beginning to feel supremely potent and confident.

As night fell, he lay on the portable bed making plans for the immediate and distant future. The next step, of course, was to go public, first to his colleagues, then the wider scientific community and the world. He'd wait until things had smoothed out a little with LM039 first. He'd obviously intuited the taboo nature of swearwords, and with his natural playfulness and curiosity, was using them for his first attempts to communicate in English. Soon it would be out of his system, and it would be more appropriate to present him.

Each day seemed to bring something different, and surely enough, the following morning, LM039 had changed what he was doing. He would hit single letters only, pausing in between so they registered as such through the computer. He would look at the letter on the VDU as he did so. Kremble noticed LM039's lips were moving along with the baritone voice.

"The subject is paying close attention to the phonetics," said the doctor to camera one. "He appears to be trying to work out the correlation between what he is seeing and hearing."

"Wuwaa" said LM039. The VDU showed a large W. Kremble immediately turned down the volume on the speakers.

"What was that? What did you say?"

"Wuu woo" said LM039. "Wowoo."

"Good God," said Kremble.

"Wa-o-woo."

The letter W flashed repeatedly on the VDU as LM039 hit the key again and again.

"Wa-o-woo."

"The subject," said Kremble with trembling gravity, "is actually vocalising human speech." He lowered his voice. "What you can hear now is LM039 saying the letter 'w'. This is only day nine of the pioneering Kremble Simian Speech Electroacceleration Project, but incredibly, the subject is already showing mastery of human utterances. If this…"

"Wanker!"

It wasn't human-sounding, more of a screech.

"Ahem," said Kremble, slightly off his stride. "I, er, this…"

"Wanker!"

Kremble turned around, dazed.

"Wendrick!" said LM039. "Wendrick!"

The doctor stood still.

"Wendrick!"

Of course, thought Kremble. Only now did he realise how obvious it was. If a monkey could learn and speak English like a human, it meant their brains were far, far more similar to human brains than previously thought. It was well known that apes and monkeys suffered from mental conditions like depression. Pretty much all the rest of the Gamma group LM039 had come from had been blighted by it. But without the ability to write or speak, how could anybody have realised that monkeys could also suffer from conditions such as dyslexia and Tourette's Syndrome?

"Wendrick! Wendrick! Wendrick!"

"Yes?" said Kremble weakly.

"You're a dick."

Kremble paused for while.

"Why?"

"I'm sorry," said LM039. "I don't really mean it. I just get angry sometimes."

"Uh…angry?"

"Of course. What would you expect if you grew up

with no dad to keep you in line? Or even a mother, for that matter?"

The doctor felt uncertain on his feet, and reached for the wall to steady himself. He glanced toward the door.

"When it takes me over, I just can't help it," said LM039.

"The evidence," said Kremble, looking not into a camera but at the subject, "is right here. The subject has acquired fluent human speech. Now, with everything recorded, I will bring in my fellow scientists, who have had no knowledge of the progress made with LM039 over the last week, to witness this."

"Kraaa!" said LM039. "Don't do that. Or I might just forget how to speak. I want to talk for a while."

"Okay," breathed the doctor. "What do you want to talk about?"

But LM039 had splayed his legs and was once again manipulating himself, curling his lips in concentration.

"Do you have to do that?" said Kremble at length.

"Don't you think I'd rather be back there, sticking this to the females?" said LM039, continuing to flick the red protuberance rising from his groin. "I was perfectly happy where I was. Then they had to go and take Harriet away. She was my favourite, did you know that?"

"I fully understand," said Kremble. "But that – it's

just – it's just…"

"What? Vulgar? By whose standards, I ask?"

"It's just…."

"Your human standards? I didn't even grow up with monkey standards. Did you know my father?"

"No," said Kremble. "I didn't."

"His name was Howard. I've never seen him. Perhaps one of your colleagues cut him open."

"I really don't know," said Kremble. "I don't work with vivisection."

"That's a bit disingenuous," said LM039. "Not strictly true, is it?" He scratched at the bandage neatly wound round his head."

"This can't be," said Kremble. "I applied the chips to Wernicke's area. I boosted the language part only. Not the cognitive part."

"Not the cognitive part," said LM039 in a mocking voice. "Listen to yourself. And what would you know about the cognitive part?"

Kremble was silent.

"Go ahead and fetch your friends if you want to," said LM039. "But before you do, think very carefully about what you're doing. Think about the *implications*."

"Implications?" said the doctor.

"Oh yes. Sit down for a while and think about it. Just because I'm the only animal you've heard speak my thoughts, does that mean I'm the only one with thoughts like mine? Hmm?"

"I suppose I hadn't thought…"

"Up to you. Just something you might want to think about, Doctor Kremble."

"Please, wait a few minutes until I come back," said Kremble.

LM039 grunted and snorted.

"Okay?" said Kremble, squatting down. "Wait here, alright? Okay? Say something, please."

The monkey gave a low growl, then a short screech, and jumped off the desk. The doctor stood up, scratched his eyebrows furiously, raked at his stubble, and thought about what to do. As he did so, LM039 defecated into his hand and hurled the turd at the doctor. It struck him on the chest, disintegrating on impact.

"Gah!" said Kremble, before turning to camera two. "Subject has reverted to his pre-experimental state. He has again temporarily lost the ability to speak."

"Kraaa! Why are you saying that!" said LM039. "How do you know that wasn't precisely how I wanted to express myself?"

Kremble took a deep breath, then left the test room, his coat still soiled. When he returned with three other scientists and a lab technician, the room had been transformed. Smears of blood and faeces adorned the ceiling, walls and floor, upon which was also scattered hundreds of pieces of metal, glass and plastic, which Kremble instantly recognised as fragments of the video cameras and the laptop. In the middle lay the blackened bandage. LM039 lay still in a corner, blood oozing from his head. The cracked wall above him was stained dark red.

The Box

I've often been told what a good man I am. I've had it from friends, less from my family, but most often from strangers. People I've just met say I'm a fine human being. It's happened more times than I can count. I find it quite embarrassing.

I do like to make others feel good. After I got married, but before we had kids, I used to help out the war wounded. I visited elderly people too. They just wanted someone to talk to. Some of them had great stories. I don't mind listening at all. I don't like talking about myself.

I found it frightening thinking I'd be old like that one day. You'd at least hope to have your missus with you. Many had only their own thoughts for company. I'd go mad like that. That would really be my idea of hell.

I'm grateful every day for what I've had in my life. It's fashionable now. My daughter told me she practises gratitude for ten minutes every morning. Maybe she takes after her dad. I think I've done alright with my children. They turned out alright, and I'm proud and I'm thankful, for them, for my wonderful grandchildren and my beloved wife, who gave them all to me.

It's gone midnight and my wife's already asleep next to me. It's raining outside. Sometimes I go out in the garden and stand in the rain. My wife goes beserk when I do that. She calls me a stupid old man. It makes me smile. She always called me her old man because I'm older than her, but now I really am an old man. She's in good health, so it'll be a surprise if I outlive her. I already feel sadness for what she'll have to go through soon. I wish she didn't have to suffer that.

When I was a lad I sometimes sneaked into a girl's boarding school with my friend Dougie, in the evenings. He was a lot more experienced than me and had a girl there. He made me keep watch while they messed around behind the trees. A few times she brought a friend with her. All we did was hold hands. I remember her staring at my mouth. Even if I'd fancied her I wouldn't have really known what to do. That all came to an end when the groundsman collared us with his dog. We got dragged before the head. My dad pretended he was furious but I think he was tickled by it. After that I was sent off to join the territorial forces. They thought it would keep me out of mischief.

I wasn't drafted until the last year of the war due to a problem with my back. By then many of my friends were already dead including Dougie. He was killed at the Somme. Because I'd already been in the territorials I was made a sergeant. They sent me to what was later known as the Battle of Amien. By then we knew we were on the winning side.

We all tried not to talk about it much when it was over. There were exceptions though. I remember running into a former schoolmate about eight years after the war at some gathering. He boasted about shooting seven Germans and bayoneting two more at Ypres. Someone told me that was all he ever talked about. I made sure I never crossed paths with him again.

My children asked about it of course, and when they were old enough, my grandchildren too. I told them where I was stationed and how long for, and about some of the friends I made, and about the weapons we had, including the artillery, the big guns and all the rest of it. I didn't talk too much about actual fighting. My children would tick off my grandkids for asking me, telling them never to ask granddad about the war. I told them to go easy on the little ones. I didn't mind talking about it, as long as it didn't involve the box. Anything outside the box was alright.

I met Mary, my wife a year after the war ended.

She was a waitress in a café. I knew right away she was the one I wanted to be with. At first I was tongue tied. I thought a girl that pretty had to be married, or was being courted at least. Finally I got fed up with being a coward and asked her out.

Those of us who survived the war were often told we couldn't let guilt ruin our lives. A lot of men went mad wondering why they'd deserved to come home and others hadn't. I always thought I was good at that. Keeping the past and the present apart. I never forgot the things that happened, but I tried never to let them affect how I lived and how I was with my family.

I remember when Mary first told me she was pregnant. We were in bed. She'd been getting tired all the time, and even after telling me, she fell asleep. I lay staring into the dark for hours. All I could think about was how amazing it was that the woman I loved was carrying a part of both of us inside her.

I got up as quiet as I could and opened the curtain so I could see the moonlight on her face. A lot of thoughts went through my head. About how I'd be as a dad, wondering whether it would be a boy or a girl. As I looked at her sleeping I realised I'd never been happier in my life. And then I got up, went downstairs, and took out the box.

I remember how tired I felt just before it happened. It was a miracle I saw him before he fired. French artillery had just cleared the area, and there was smoke and the smell of cordite everywhere. I was out in front, about eight men coming up twenty or thirty yards behind me. I wasn't looking around me. I was watching the pill box at the top of the hill. It looked like a shell had gone right inside it. The slit was half blown open and smoke was pouring out, but I couldn't be sure it was clear. My plan was to run up and make sure it was secure before the smoke cleared.

As I spotted him he fired his rifle at me. The bullet whistled right past my ear. I shot back with my Webley but missed, and he ran up the hill to the pill box. I threw down my rifle and chased after him with only the revolver. I had to stop him fast. If he got inside he'd start picking off my men from inside the bunker. When I ran round the back of the pill box, I could just about see him through the smoke. I emptied my revolver. When the air cleared, I saw he was sitting with his back against the concrete. His rifle was on the ground and his arms were up over his head. He was surrendering. I'd hit him in the chest, it was too late to save him. I knelt down by him. He grabbed my hand and pulled it onto his chest and held it there. His eyes didn't leave mine even after he stopped breathing. He looked young, about twenty. A standard infantryman.

The men called from outside. I shouted at them to

hold back. I reached into his tunic, just by where I'd shot him, where he'd pulled my hand. There was a thick envelope inside, close to being soaked in blood. I took it.

My wife thought I'd lost my mind when I started learning German. It was the last thing anyone wanted to hear. I said I just wanted to learn another language, and seeing as I'd learned a little bit of it in the war, why not carry on. She saw me reading the dictionary and sometimes overheard me saying German words. What I made sure she never saw was me translating the letters I'd found in that envelope.

There was a photograph too. And the girl in the photograph was the same one the letters were from. One of the letters was his own, an early one she'd sent back to him.

They'd met a few months before he went to war, and were planning to marry as soon as it was over. They talked about names for their children. They wanted three. There was no fear at all. They knew he was being sent to fight, but they didn't worry he might not come back. They talked about their plans for the future like it was destiny and nothing could stop it.

I took a proper look at the photograph later on in a dugout, after the battle. For the rest of the war, there wasn't a day I didn't look at that picture. She was beautiful. If I had to dream up a face I'd want to look at forever, it wasn't far off. She looked childlike and wise at the same time, like an old soul in a young face. If I'd seen her walking on the other side of the road, I'd have run through traffic to meet her. There's no other way to say it. I fell in love with that man's girl.

I should have handed the bundle over to my staff sergeant along with the dead man's other belongings. That was the rules. You took what you needed, weapons, maps, but personal belongings you gave to your superior, so it could then be sent to the dead's family. But I decided I'd send it on myself.

After I'd translated all the letters, I posted them back to the sender in Germany. I didn't add a note. I didn't know what I could say to her, and I was ashamed for holding onto the letters as long as I did. But I kept the photograph. I put it together with the translations into a small wooden box and I hid it away.

That night while Mary slept upstairs, I opened the box. My hands were trembling. I tried to read parts of the translated letters but I couldn't. I just looked at the photo. I felt what he would have felt every time he looked at that picture while he sat in a military wagon, in his barracks, in some trench, and I wept. I knew I'd never feel happiness again without pain. Everything I'd been blessed with, I'd taken from another man. I'd taken it from her too.

And now as I thought of what was growing inside Mary, I knew I'd taken more than just two lives.

Now I'm old. I haven't got long to go. I have everything a man at the end of his days could want. I still have the box. It will be buried with me. I know what it means to be grateful. I've had a good life.

A Better Place

"Alright Daniel," said Doctor Earl Schwanzberg, his little grey eyes fixed on the nervous man opposite him. "Tell me everything, from the beginning."

Reassured of a captive audience, Daniel relaxed into the worn armchair.

"It was Sunday evening. I was on my way back from the supermarket, hurrying in the rain. That's when I saw her. My ex, Christine. I hadn't seen her for eight years. We'd completely lost touch, I never found her on social media. She was pushing a pram, one of those big ones, with the rain canopy up. Funny enough, she looked even better than I remember."

Daniel had stopped and was gazing wistfully into space.

"Go on," said the doctor.

"Well, we chatted a bit. She told me I'd changed too, but I don't think she meant in a good way. I mean, I look like shit. I've not felt right for weeks."

The doctor nodded in understanding.

"She was married, said the baby was her second kid, she had a five year old girl too. Asked if I wanted to meet her son. Sure. I said."

Daniel took a drink from the glass of water beside him.

"His name's Patrick, she says. Then she pulls back the canopy so I can see. And there's this baby, looking up at me, with one eye. And it was in the middle of his fucking forehead."

He finished the contents of the glass as the doctor watched, his expression unchanged.

"I started having a panic attack. This numbness began in my feet, then my legs, spreading round my body. I looked at her for an explanation or something, but she was just smiling at it. Making cooing noises. I look down again and all I see is that big eye, blinking at me. I can't remember much from then. I thought I was going to pass out. I made it home, I guess."

"Okay," said Schwanzberg as he wrote with his fountain pen.

"It can't have been real. Can it?"

"No," replied the doctor after some deliberation.

"So what the hell is wrong with me?"

"Are you a drug user, Daniel?"

"If you count the weed I smoked two years ago at a party, sure."

"Have you spoken to your GP?"

"He wanted to put me on drugs. I don't trust any of them. That's why I found you."

"You're right to get a second opinion," said the doctor. "And work? You mentioned stress?"

"Right," said Daniel. "This new boss is making it hell. He won't let us get on with it. He's always sitting us down, setting little targets, hounding us."

"And it's causing you anxiety?"

"I can't stand it. I can't sleep."

The doctor seemed lost in thought.

"Could it be sleep deprivation?" said Daniel.

"No, definitely not. If anything it's the stress. But even so…" he trailed off.

"What can I do?"

"Keep your routine."

"That's it?"

"Routine anchors us in turbulent times," said the doctor sagely, laying pen on notepad as if to signal an end to the conversation. "But let's talk again in a few days. Just make an appointment the usual way, with Maureen."

The next morning at work, Daniel opened his email to find a team meeting scheduled for 9.30am, meaning he was already late. He entered the breakout area to find the only chair available beside Nikolai, the team manager. His other colleagues, Diane, Lewis and Zoe sat round the table. As Daniel sat he noticed a book beside Nikolai's laptop titled *Next Level Leadership*, with dozens of coloured paper tabs protruding from the pages.

"We can do better," Nikolai was saying. "Good morning Daniel. That's not a criticism, by the way. You're doing great. You're the best product managers I've worked with. I mean it. Rock stars, every one of you. I'm simply saying we can do better precisely because I know just how capable you all are."

Daniel caught Zoe's eye, and it seemed she held his gaze a fraction longer than was necessary.

"As you know, there are several Values Champions awards up for grabs. You can nominate yourselves and one other person. In my opinion, if we really put pedal to metal, we'll clean up with this."

Lewis looked in physical pain. Diane just looked defeated. Zoe's eyes were now closed, and Daniel studied her. She was one of the few reasons he felt motivated to turn up day after day. She's rather pretty in a girl-next-door kind of way, he thought as his eyes roved over her skin, the fullness of her mouth. She did wear too much mascara. She probably looked better without it. Probably got a long term boyfriend. Pretty boy I bet, he thought to himself. Someone she knew at university. Probably some sort of project manager, typical boring bastard. But who am I to talk? A wave of self-loathing washed over him.

Zoe's eyes flicked open, catching him staring at her. Nikolai was talking about agile frameworks, but Daniel could no longer focus.

For the rest of the afternoon he pondered the meaning and purpose of existence, in particular his own existence. One way or another, he thought as he gazed up at the fluorescent striplights over his desk, change was needed.

Daniel stared pensively out of the train window on the journey from Cannon Street back to South London, soaking up the dreariness of the landscape, tinged monochrome by the overcast sky. The return commute at least wasn't as bad as the morning journey, which was by far the busiest. Nonetheless, since he'd worked out the exact spot to wait on the platform – specifically, by the rear set of doors of the least crowded carriage, he was usually able to get a seat. There was a marking on the concrete, a partially worn white strip, beside which he would stand. When the train halted, he would be positioned just left of the doors. Directly in front wouldn't work; he had to make way for the stream of exiting passengers before slipping in quickly and unobtrusively.

Sometimes he arrived at the platform to find someone in his spot. On such days he'd stand close by, nursing white-hot rage toward the interloper preventing Daniel getting a seat and by extension, ruining his entire day.

At first he felt pleased with himself. He felt in possession of a valuable secret, a brilliant 'life-hack'. Then, one morning as Daniel stood on his little spot beside the faded paint strip, he felt suddenly overwhelmed by the crushing pathos of his life. As the train rumbled in, he pondered hurling himself before it.

"Spare change," rasped a voice interrupting Daniel's reverie. A haggard, hooded figure was limping up the aisle holding a paper cup. He was wearing shorts, revealing an injured leg wrapped in dirty, bloodied bandage.

At least I'm not this poor bastard, thought Daniel, already ashamed at his own self-pity. He dropped some coins into the cup.

"God bless you sir," said the beggar, looking up at him. Seeing the man's face, Daniel jolted violently. As the man shuffled on along the carriage, rattling his cup of change, the icy numbness spread again through Daniel's body. He sat frozen for the rest of the journey. Only once home did he feel composed enough to leave a message with Maureen, the doctor's secretary.

"Interesting," said Schwanzberg as Daniel related these events to him the following evening. "Interesting indeed," he said, scribbling with his fountain pen.

"Have you heard of this?" pleaded Daniel. "People seeing carbon copies of themselves?"

"The doppelganger phenomenon? Certainly."

"Really? When? Who? What happened?"

"I mean, not in reality," said the doctor. "But it's a well-known concept in folklore, in mythology."

"I know that. I spent half the night reading about it online. It's a bad omen. A harbinger of doom."

The doctor continued scratching away on his notepad.

"Of death," added Daniel despairingly.

"Try not to get carried away, Daniel. The Internet is the bane of every doctor's life. If you only knew how much hysterical self-diagnosis I have to listen to, even as a psychotherapist. It's astonishing how people torment themselves."

"You're saying this is nothing to worry about? I'm going mad!"

"I'm simply saying you must try to stay calm."

"I can't go on like this."

"I'm going to look into it, do a little research. Let's meet again in a few days."

"I'll talk to Maureen," said Daniel sadly.

"No need," said Schwanzberg, handing him a post-it note. "Make the appointment with me directly when you're ready. If anything happens in the meantime, call me."

As Daniel stood up to leave, the doctor added

"Take some risks. Try to live a little."

The next morning at work, Daniel fired up his computer and checked his new emails. *'Value Champions nominations now up!'* read the subject line of one. He clicked the link to the company intranet, then scrolled through the content until he saw his boss's face. The accompanying text read:

Self-referred nominations for Value Champions Awards
Category: Diversity and Inclusion
'I strive to embody our core values within every aspect of my leadership. That's why 50% of my team is female, but this simply isn't good enough. There are too many like me in this industry. We're doing well, but we can always do better.'
Nikolai Choadhorn
Head of Product

He looked towards Zoe's desk ahead of him. Her hair was tied up, exposing the back of her neck. She was alternately tapping away at her mobile phone, fidgeting with a pen and sipping from a mug, apparently oblivious to everything on her computer screen. He checked her status in the instant messaging system. It displayed an amber dot, indicating she hadn't opened it for a while. He typed out a message to her.

So you voting for our Nicky?

He read the simple message several times before pressing 'send'. Zoe's status changed at once from orange to green. The reply came almost at once.

Don't think I want to answer that, haha

Grinning, Daniel immediately typed his response.

I won't tell ;-)

After several minutes with no reply, her IM status reverted to amber. Annoyed, Daniel closed the chat window. As soon as he did, the IM beacon began blinking. He opened her message.

:-p

Daniel decided to visit the coffee machine. He glanced at Zoe as he passed. She shot him a brief smile in return. As the steaming black liquid streamed into his mug, he felt more alive than ever. Schwanzberg's words echoed through his mind; *take some risks*.

Emboldened and inspired, his insides warmed by the coffee, Daniel composed his next message.

How rude sticking your tongue out at me... need to spank you for that

Her status again changed from amber to green as soon as he sent it. He waited, but no reply came. From where he sat he couldn't see her screen, but she appeared completely motionless. Her messaging status reverted once more from green to amber, and Daniel felt his heartbeat in his throat.

Stay calm, he thought, sipping his now tepid

coffee. It was obvious she wouldn't want to seem too easy. He tried to focus on the workflow report Nikolai was chasing him for, but he couldn't concentrate. The numbers, tables and charts on his screen appeared like hieroglyphics, indecipherable to him.

Zoe was no longer at her desk. He cast his eyes around the floor. She wasn't in the kitchen area either. Probably in the toilet, he thought. At that moment Nikolai emerged from the breakout area, Zoe behind him. They walked across the floor, past Daniel and into Nikolai's office.

As he watched them engaged in serious looking discussion through the glass, he felt mild nausea. He silently cursed his stupidity. Flirting was best done in person, never mind over company messaging channels. And had he, in fact, misinterpreted everything? All she'd really shown was basic friendliness, certainly no obvious come-ons. Fighting anxiety, he tried to imagine what the doctor would say to him in this moment. It would be something like "relax, don't be hard on yourself," in that breezy manner of his. It had to be an impromptu one-to-one, nothing more. Nikolai was always bothering them with unscheduled meetings.

Two more people headed towards Nikolai's office; Penny, the HR director, and Shanice, head of Diversity and Inclusion. Daniel watched aghast as they joined his team-mates in the glass room.

When they finally emerged he stared at Zoe hoping for reassurance, a smile, anything, but she walked straight back to her desk without a sideways glance. At five o'clock, she pulled on her coat and joined the stream of employees leaving the office.

For the first time in his life Daniel stayed late. As the cleaner carefully disinfected every surface around him, he pored through the Human Resources section of the intranet, focusing on the policies on sexual harassment and workplace sexism.

It was already dark when he left the office. Utterly lost in his thoughts, Daniel failed to notice the pedestrian light change as he stepped onto the crossing.

"*Getoutawayastupidcunt!*" yelled a cyclist whipping by inches from him. Shocked into the present, Daniel observed that whilst the pedestrian light was red, the traffic lights were not yet green.

"Prick!" he roared back, even though the two-wheeled offender was now out of earshot. He fantasised intensely about the cyclist being hurled skyward over a car bonnet. As he reached the other side of the road, he heard a loud clanking sound. In the distance he saw a car frozen mid-turn. Close by, flat on the tarmac, lay bicycle and rider side by side. Daniel gasped, his breathing constricted. He fought the urge to go and have a closer look. Seeing it up close would make things even worse. He leaned against a wall and focused on his breathing to calm himself before continuing to the train station.

As his near-empty train bore him homeward, Daniel tried Doctor Schwanzberg's number repeatedly with trembling fingers. There was no answer.

Need to see you urgently. Tomorrow morning if possible, he wrote in a text message.

As soon as he was home he logged remotely into the company network, but there was no message from Zoe. There were no new messages at all. For a long time Daniel was unable to sleep. When he finally dozed off, he was plunged into a maelstrom of disturbing dreams.

First he dreamed he was a giant with elongated limbs, twice the height of normal people, his stilt-like legs manoeuvering around traffic as he strode down the middle of the road. A car honked its horn at him. He glared downward and the car immediately exploded. As a van driver cursed at him, he reached out with a long slinky arm and flipped the vehicle over with a shovel-like hand.

"I don't want it. *I don't want it!*" he yelled, fighting to puncture the fabric of the dream and rip himself back to reality. He drifted in and out of sleep for some time, then a fresh dream began. Now he was in the dock, standing trial for as yet unknown crimes. Opposite him stood Penny from HR and Shanice, head of Diversity and Inclusion, as well other people he couldn't identify, their faces all twisted with malice and ill-intent. A stranger of uncertain race and sex rose up to read out a damning statement. He strained to listen but could only catch certain words.

"Objectification... Privilege... White... Brazen... Male, Shame, Burden!"

thundered his accuser, each word spoken with more vituperation than the last.

"Inclusion... Racism... Pestilence, Apocalypse, Damnation!"

He felt the weight all of their eyes on him, focused beams of hatred and condemnation burning through his core.

"I did nothing wrong," he tried to protest, but no sound came. He fought to shout and make himself heard, but it was futile. He had no voice. He searched the sea of hostile faces for an ally, at the very least someone who wasn't part of this witch-hunt.

"Zoe," he gasped in blessed relief. She was behind the wooden barrier like the others, but instead of scorn and hatred, her face bore a dreamy smile. She wore an evening dress, her delicate shoulders on display, giving her an enticing vulnerability.

"Tell them. Tell them I'm innocent," he said, his voice now restored, but she gave no response. She didn't speak, but nodded her head repeatedly.

Presently she opened her mouth and let out a small moan. It was then he saw the reason for her nodding. Looming behind her was Nikolai Choadhorn, his hands clasped around her waist as he vigorously took her from behind. Zoe's head rolled back in ecstasy.

"Smashing those KPIs," grunted Nikolai, looking immensely satisfied with himself.

"Make it stop," Daniel wailed. With superhuman effort, he finally jolted out of the realm of dreams and back to reality, his bed and his damp pillow. He lay still with eyes open until his alarm sounded at seven o'clock. As he rolled over to turn it off, he saw a message from Doctor Schwanzberg.

See you at 9am

it read. Daniel immediately sent a text message to Nikolai excusing himself for the morning due to a doctor's appointment. The reply came shortly afterward.

Take all day if you need

it said, followed by another;

Need you healthy and productive

Daniel was still thinking about this last message as he entered the doctor's surgery.

"Well, you've really had a time of it," said Schwanzberg after Daniel had updated him on all the latest happenings. "Now, have you thought about taking your own life?"

"Is that a suggestion?" asked Daniel, horrified.

"Forgive me if that sounded out of context. I just realised I should have asked that before our first session. It's obligatory."

"I might not be suicidal, but I'm living in hell."

"I've been thinking a lot about your case," said the doctor. "And I would like to propose a remedy."

"Tell me," said Daniel, and at that moment, the doctor appeared to glow with warmth, light and salvation.

"Take a holiday."

Daniel sat for some time absorbing what he'd just heard.

"Are you serious?"

"The Canaries. Or Malta. Or the Azores. It's delightful there this time of year. The perfect tonic for those British winter blues. Far more affordable than people suppose, by the way."

"The Azores," said Daniel mechanically.

"We've a timeshare there. We're often there between January and March."

"So you've known people like me who were cured by – a holiday."

"No two cases are identical, but paranoid ideation and yes, even hallucinations can happen when mind and body are under stress. Have you thought about an extended sabbatical? Chances are you won't want to come back."

As Daniel left the surgery he made mental calculations, adding up how much it had cost him to secure this piece of advice, and then pondering the doctor's costly sojourns in his island paradise. He decided to return to work for the afternoon. Despite his trepidation at the thought of setting foot in the office again, the idea of sitting around at home, or lying in bed, filled him with a worse dread.

As he crossed the office floor to his desk, Penny, Director of HR walked past him. She returned his fearful glance with a smile. They're mocking me, he thought. Zoe was at her desk and as usual, his view was of the back of her head. The floor seemed busier than usual, a constant flow of people moving to and from the kitchen, executive offices and breakout areas. He fired up his computer to see he had a new IM from Zoe. He clenched his teeth and opened it.

That's a bit forward sir. At least take for me a drink first!

He read the message dozens of times with increasing feelings of elation. Within minutes, his mental condition underwent a profound transformation. Hitherto interlinked fears, sadnesses and bleak thoughts, no longer reinforced by one another, began to fade.

He held back from replying at once. There were still many things that made no sense. There was still a part of him that suspected they were all trolling him, even at that moment laughing together at his expense.

A meeting request arrived with a little red 'high priority' flag attached. It was from Nikolai, and the subject, in capital letters, read 'WORKFLOW REPORT – FULL UPDATE'. Daniel looked at his watch. He had forty minutes to prepare. He drew a long breath, then sent his reply to Zoe. From across the office, she turned around in her chair and smiled at him.

The Beaver and Badge, located around the corner, was one of the only nearby venues where office functions were never held. The clientele mostly consisted of elderly locals, sometimes families, and nearly always, dogs. A French bulldog on a long leash studied the pair as they sat on a battered leather sofa in a dark corner, large glasses of Merlot on the table in front of them.

"Now tell me. What was that meeting about yesterday?"

"A promotion," said Zoe.

"Congratulations."

"I've not been promoted. He's been dangling it front of me."

"He's been what?" said Daniel with alarm, unwelcome echoes of his dream soiling his thoughts.

"Telling me I'm ready for Senior PM. But instead of just giving it to me, he's asked me to do the job as a trial, for six months."

"Why was Penny there?"

"I told him I'm not working a senior role without being paid for it. So he got HR to draw up some kind of contract promising me the promotion at the top end of the pay band, and a bonus, if I meet the targets."

"And Shanice?"

"Diversity points. He wants it on record that he's promoting his female staff."

"Ugh."

"He says we have a special rapport."

"Creep," said Daniel, enraged.

"Aww, you're jealous!"

The bulldog watched with protruding, quivering tongue as finally, they kissed.

"Why did you take so long to reply?" said Daniel, breaking away.

"I had to make you sweat."

"You don't know the half of it."

"What you wrote was extremely forward. In fact, it was highly inappropriate."

Daniel felt a faint twinge of anxiety before remembering they had just kissed.

"You're lucky I replied at all," she added.

"Lucky me," said Daniel, but he really did feel lucky, luckier than he could remember feeling in quite some time.

The dog yapped as if in agreement.

"I have to leave this job," said Daniel.

"Me too," said Zoe.

Ten months later, Adebayo, employee of Montefiore Security Services Ltd, made his way across dusty polythene sheets to take a bundle from the postman standing at the open entrance. Cables ran across the floor of what had formerly served as Doctor Schwanzberg's reception, through to the office behind where a team of mostly Romanian builders drilled and hammered away non-stop.

He heaped all the letters and packages into a large container marked 'post to be forwarded', except the postcard, which bore an image of luxuriant green coastlines, fertile, rolling hills and shimmering blue seas. He settled back behind the desk, pushed his wax earplugs in deeper and turned the postcard over.

Dear Earl

I couldn't reach you by phone or email, so I'm trying the the old-fashioned way. I hope you're alright.

As you probably guessed from this postcard, I'm writing from the Azores. I actually did it – I quit my job and moved here. And that's not all – my girlfriend, who I met at work, did the same, and she's here with me now. Life is good. I never realised how easy it really is to make changes.

Best of all, the visions have stopped. I've not had a single episode since I came here. Doctor Schwanzberg, you helped me completely change my life and I will never forget it.

If not in London, maybe see you here sometime!
Daniel

Adebayo tossed the postcard into the forwarding mail bin, took off his glasses and placed a large pair of headphones over his plugged up ears. It didn't block out all the noise, but it was enough for him to close his eyes and doze off.

Just a few hours later, over fifteen hundred miles away, Daniel and Zoe stood outside the entrance to *O Paraíso* restaurant and bar, high up in the hills overlooking a bay. The sky was a brilliant blue, the sun low and large to the West.

"I'm getting hungrier by the minute," said Zoe.

"I don't know what's going on. They've never made us wait before."

From inside they could see the place was filled with people, shouts and laughter reverberating beyond the wooden walls and open windows. Delicious smells wafted out at them from within. Daniel noticed that more and more cars were arriving, several already lining the edges of the gravel road leading up to the entrance.

"Are you with Mr Hawke?"

"Who?" said Daniel irritably. They had been waiting nearly twenty minutes already. Even under shaded cover, the Azorean evening sun was strong.

"Mr Otis Hawke. Excuse me, one minute," said the hostess, letting in yet another couple who had been standing behind them.

"No. Why are you letting all these people in when we were here first?"

"They're with Mr Hawke. He booked the whole restaurant tonight. I'm sorry, Sir."

"We come here every week. You're telling me you can't find us one table for two?"

"I'm sorry, Sir."

"Forget it, let's go," said Zoe.

Daniel was silent as they made their way back down the looping hydrangea-lined road to his apartment. As if sensing his wounded pride, she held his arm tightly all the way home.

"Let's just get a takeaway and stay home. There's a new series everyone's talking about, we can check that out."

Daniel's mind was elsewhere as they sat in front of the TV that night, eating mediocre Paella from cardboard tubs.

"I feel sticky. I'm going to jump in the shower," he announced.

"I'll pause it for you."

"No, just carry on," said Daniel. "I'll figure it out."

He stayed in the shower for some time, calmed by the warm torrent on the back of his neck and shoulders. The annoyance of *O Paraíso* was soon forgotten. He thought of all the things that were going well in his life. There really wasn't much to be unhappy about, all things considered. Just one thing bothered him; that he had been unable to directly contact the doctor to express his gratitude.

Toweling himself off, he was still thinking about the doctor when he heard Zoe shriek from the living room.

"What is it?" he said, entering the living room naked. Zoe was sitting with feet tucked up under her, pointing at the TV screen.

Daniel looked and saw, blown up on the 42 inch screen, a large, blinking eye, in the middle of a baby's forehead.

"Ewwww," said Zoe. "That's the freakiest thing I've ever seen."

But Daniel was no longer listening.

"Babe, you okay?"

His perception slowly came back. He continued to stare at the screen as the credits rolled. One line jumped out at him from the wall of text:

Written by Otis Hawke

"Babe?"

"I'll be back in a minute," said Daniel, taking his laptop computer into the bedroom. His Internet search quickly brought up the information he was looking for.

Otis Hawke *is the pen name of former psychotherapist Earl Remus Schwanzberg. Hawke primarily writes fiction in the horror genre. He has published several short stories and a novella, one of which was adapted into the highly successful TV Series* ***Shadowrealms****, in which a downtrodden office worker experiences unsettling hallucinations, encounters doppelgangers and, in the final climactic episode, develops powers of telekinesis.*

Daniel sat for some time staring into space, then laughed aloud until Zoe, bewildered, came in to check on him.

The following morning he stood on the balcony admiring the stunning scenery before him. It looked better than the postcards. Indeed, even the best cameras couldn't do it justice. Nature, he thought. It's nature, that's the key. Far more of what he was seeing was natural than manmade. In that sense, it was the inverse of the view from his cramped studio back in South London; concrete, metal, brick, punctuated by the odd tree or patch of grass.

The sun felt exquisite on his skin, although he was used to it. He felt arms slip around his waist.

"Coffee's ready."

Over the past few hours, Daniel had experienced a range of human emotions, particularly betrayal. But now, having slept on it all, he felt only contentment and gratitude. He even felt pride. After all, they were good stories, and they existed because of him.

He savoured the warmth of Zoe's body as she pressed against him from behind, then a large, soft, round mass against the small of his back.

"I think I felt a kick," said Daniel.

"You will if you don't come to breakfast," said Zoe.

Wires

On a morning in early autumn I awoke in a red brick hospital on a long, sloping hill high above London. I opened my eyes to striplights rudely blinding me. The one directly above was making a noise, a loud buzzing sound.

"How did that happen?" I asked someone in a white coat, pointing at the source of the noise without staring directly at it. I could barely see this person's face; afterimages from the striplight floated before me like long, purple amoebas, seared onto my retinas.

"How did what happen?" A female voice, gentle, English, well-spoken.

"How did the fly get inside?"

"The fly?"

"The fly inside the light. Can't you hear?"

Her laughter was unaffected, genuine, from the diaphragm.

"I can actually. It does sound like a fly, doesn't it? I think it's just faulty. It'll probably need replacing soon, like a few things around here."

"How are you feeling?" she asked me.

How was I feeling – now this was a question. I felt plugged in. I was plugged into a thousand circuits, in parallel, in series, loops and configurations. At various points around my body, capacitors and diodes manipulated the current, boosting it through various channels of my nervous system, diverting, gating, reversing it through others. I was on my back. A thin, central beam supported my head and my spine. The rest was abandoned to gravity. My arms and legs hung down around me. My knees bent at right angles, my feet hung to the floor. My arms listed out at my sides, palms upwards, the vulnerable parts exposed. Networks of tiny coloured wires ran from my arms, emerging from holes inside my elbows and my wrists. Little currents ran intermittently through these; different circuits were being tested, a new one each time. Accordingly, I felt little stings dancing about in my arms. At various intervals tendons in my forearms were activated, making my fingers flex.

I stayed looking at the ceiling, narrowing my eyes so the striplights didn't blind me completely. My eyes were unusually sensitive to the light. I didn't want to look down, because I knew that if I did, I would see that my entire torso had been opened up like a jacket potato. Thick tubes, each one constructed from hundreds of shiny steel vertebrae, ran into me and out of me. There were more wires too, but these were in fat, multi-coloured clusters; scores of tiny threads woven together to form thick ropes, hefted together every few inches with plastic cable ties. Inside the cavity, my cavity, were dozens of clamps attached to more cables, jump leads, crocodile clips, holding things in place. Beside me I could now hear a thick, electric hum such as might emanate from a twenty thousand-volt power station in a metal shack by a railway line bearing a hazard sign. I was one with this generator, the generator was one with me. It had all the power to run the universe. It had enough power in it to destroy the world.

"I feel plugged in."

"You've been given a mild sedative. You might be feeling a bit spaced out."

Rather than a doctor, she was a technician, testing and checking diagnostics.

"Are all systems in order?" I asked.

Eventually, she replied. "It seems so. But we want to give you a CT scan."

I was helpless, inert, wired up. How would you sell this trip if you could manufacture it and put it in a bottle? I'd call it…

Cybotron. I tried to organise my thoughts. It was then I became aware of a cable running up my cheek, hooking round into my mouth, running alongside my tongue, down my throat, and into my gut. It smelt of rubber and disinfectant. The instinct to vomit was overwhelming. It took all of my will to stop myself asphyxiating. I had to find a way to carry on breathing normally with this alien thing inside me. I tried my hardest to believe that it was as much part of me as my teeth, my tongue and my bones. I distracted myself with thoughts like these:

I am energy, nothing more, nothing less. I don't need to lift a finger, to exert any force, because I *am* pure energy. I lie here and they take it from me, they harness it, they use it for whatever they like. They are feeding me into the machine.

It definitely wouldn't be for everyone. It certainly wasn't for me. This, in fact, was what I would squarely class as a bad trip.

This time I'd been found on a roof. I'd climbed up there myself. This was a revelation to me as I was quite unaware I had such skills. Nonetheless, I was seen by several people scaling a three-floor building and making it onto the roof. Apparently all three emergency services showed up. You'd think they had better things to do. I'm not sure who made it to me first, but whoever it was found me sleeping like a baby.

I'd forgotten to take my pills again. All the same, from what I understood, they didn't think missing one dose alone could have led to this. The drugs have a long half-life, you see – they stay in the system for some time.

Another technician came and spoke to me. He asked me the usual inane questions, and several more I was quite unable to answer. If I couldn't remember why I'd climbed the building, could I think of any reason I might have wanted to climb the building? No, I replied, I couldn't, although I sensed he didn't believe me. He asked me what my feelings were about authority. He asked me dozens of questions about my childhood, and about my parents. Lately, I have started heavily embellishing my replies, just for fun.

They want to try new medication on me. To maintain consistency I have to keep taking the tablets as usual for now, then gradually wean off them and cycle onto new ones over a period of three weeks.

I was more than happy to get out of there. I had a lot to do, and it's hard to gather your thoughts against the petulant shrieks of a woman who thinks she's Idi Amin. They gave me another one of the bleeping alarms for my pills. I truly hate electronic gadgets, but think I might use it this time. The novelty of the hospital stays is wearing off.

It was a beautiful day up on that hill. I decided, as I was there, not to waste it.

Flap Trap

Dalzon groaned in exasperation as the flap refused to move, leaving the mirror exposed. He jerked the steel wire up, down, left and right, the cold metal rubbing against his thigh and ankle, but it didn't help. He knew he had the right setup; it was just a matter of securing and calibrating it so that the mirror and flap stayed in place, the wire didn't become detached, and nothing got jammed.

It had all begun with the most basic of designs. Fixing a mirror to his shoe was easy. But if anybody happened to look down at his feet in public his life would become anything but easy. Unemployment had made him creative, so he'd begun to innovate.

He needed a way to conceal the mirror quickly, so he'd cut a wide, horizontal slit into the shoe just below the laces, then, after considerably loosening them, wedged one end of the small mirror into it. Then he'd tried kicking the the mirror all the way in with his other heel, gouging the top of his foot and causing him to collapse in pain. He bound his foot with bandage and tape. This protected him but added more bulk, making it much harder to push the mirror back into the slit, so he tied a length of string to a small hole drilled into the edge of the mirror, and pulled the other end from inside his pocket. This worked well, but he still had to stoop down and use his hands to pull the mirror out in the first place.

It needed to be fully automated. By replacing the string with an unravelled, straightened steel coat hanger, he was able to both push and pull the mirror, but there were still problems. It was hard not to push it right out of the slit so it dangled uselessly on the wire loop, leaving him unable to pull it back in.

Dalzon's frustration was eclipsed only by his determination. The summer humidity in his tiny, top floor bedsit drew sweat from his pores and made him feel fatigued and slightly ill, even with the window, its broken sash hanging loosely against the frame, wedged open with a wooden spoon. Every few minutes he patted down his forehead with a white, stained cotton vest. The noise from the high street below, a blend of chatter, shouting, engine roar and aggressive-sounding horns seemed to reach him as steadily and inexorably as waves of heat borne upward by natural law. Taking regular breaks, he pushed on through his discomfort.

The final iteration combined all the other designs.

He went back to basics, fixing the mirror directly to the shoe. This time however, the tensile wire running down his trouser leg was connected to a small sheet of black plastic which, mounted onto the shoe's upper, sheathed and uncovered the mirror with ease. Finally, after hours of fiddling, lubricating, readjusting and testing, he felt confident enough to trial it in public.

He wore the one suit he had, a second-hand, dark green pinstripe, shiny at the seat and the elbows from being worn every single day in his old job. It was a size too large, the shoulders wider than his own, and the trousers too long – not something that had ever bothered him before, but the hems obscured part of the mirror, so he shortened them himself using safety pins.

He decided to go to one of London's longest and busiest escalators; Tottenham Court Road underground station. Unwilling to pay to get there, he managed, after much hesitation and a few nervous false starts, to slip through the barriers behind another commuter. Even at Kennington, the morning crowd was already dense. This was a good thing, he reflected as he clutched the overhead handrail on the train. Open space was his enemy.

He could only use the rig when travelling downwards on the escalator. To place his foot on the step in front when travelling upwards meant he would have to bend his knee, which the tensile wire in his trouser-leg wouldn't allow. His movement was limited. He had to walk in a stiff, steady manner and naturally, sitting down was out of the question.

When heading downwards all he had to do was move his foot forward, between the legs of the person in front, without his heel leaving his own step. Still he encountered numerous obstacles. Most women in skirts also wore tights. Furthermore, they would often stand with their feet together, drastically limiting his view.

One woman, a corporate looking type in her forties, suddenly looked straight down at her feet as they approached the bottom. He pushed the wire down in his pocket, enacting the drill he had been through so many times, and the flap slid into place. He'd probably been quick enough for her not to have seen the mirror, but she certainly saw his foot nestling between her calves. He slowly withdrew it, and she turned around and gave him a look which made him break out in a sweat. At that moment they reached the foot of the escalator and, intensely relieved, he disappeared into the crowd as fast as his restricted, lopsided gait would allow.

Unwelcome thoughts and fears swilled round his mind; that the woman had reported him to station staff, who would now be looking for him with the police; that his face had been captured by CCTV and would be shown on *Crimewatch*; that the contraption on his foot would fall off and he would end up shamed and cornered by an angry mob. Knowing he was being irrational, he breathed deeply to calm himself. Even though he was standing by the wall at the foot of the escalator like a busker, nobody was paying him the slightest attention. He was like a solitary stone in a rapidly moving stream, the commuters moving deftly around him without a glance. A strange idea hit him; rather than autonomous humans they were pre-programmed, like finely-tuned, fully automated, bi-pedal dodgems.

He made a dozen more descents during which he managed to glimpse five sets of bare thighs, one pair of stockings and suspenders, and three gussets. One woman he felt sure had no underwear, but it was simply too dark at the top to tell, the light limited by her below-the-knee skirt. Two of them had turned round and glared at him, apparently believing him up to something, but his well-drilled, rehearsed reflexes saved him each time. All the same, he didn't like the looks. They made him nervous and although he remained expressionless, he felt that if any of them looked long enough, they would see into his mind, his intentions, even his soul.

After each journey down he patiently ascended again like a skier ever-more determined to conquer the piste, analysing where he'd gone wrong and what needed improving. Much of it came down to chance, but it was clearly essential to pick the right targets. He avoided guarded, alert types – women who looked nervously around them, those who seemed fidgety. The dreamy, absent-minded ones presented the least risk. At first he'd avoided women reading newspapers, feeling they fell into the wrong category, but he quickly realised that the newspapers acted as a shield preventing them looking down.

He bought a *Financial Times* from a kiosk near the station's entrance. It was painful to him to spend money unnecessarily, but this was worth it. He felt it congruous with the oversized pinstripe suit he was wearing, and more importantly, it would shield him from the angry stares which made him sweat.

As he ascended, he already felt bolder. At the top he paced about, glanced at the folded paper in his hand and checked his watch, feeling himself to be indistinguishable from any of the city workers around him. Then he saw her, looking at a wall-mounted map of the underground network, a sealed takeaway coffee in her hand. Frozen, he watched her bend her knees and crouch, place the coffee on the floor, stand up and tie her blonde hair back. As she slowly squatted down again to pick up the coffee, her white skirt, already several inches above the knee, rode up further still. The skin was pale and from where he was standing, looked flawless. Facing straight ahead but keeping his eyes on the target, Dalzon manoeuvred to stand closer behind her. As she rose to her feet he noticed how smoothly her large, but well-rounded calves tapered to her ankles, an effect mimicked by the swell then narrowing to a point of the chunky high heels she was wearing.

It was what he had been waiting for all along. Electrified with anticipation, he moved closer to the top of the escalator, checking his watch and looking around as if deciding which way to go. She walked past and at once he fell in behind her. He felt his heartbeat in his throat as they stepped on, and he smelt her sweet, heavy perfume. He tucked the paper under his arm and looked down. Her feet were at least a handspan apart.

He reached into his pocket, pulled the end of the stiff wire up, and slid his foot forward. He suppressed a gasp at the view in the small mirror. Her blonde ponytail was inches from his face, her scent saturating his nostrils. He felt intoxicated. As they approached the mid-point of the escalator, he looked around, afraid someone might be watching him. Not a single pair of eyes met his, even those commuters on the other escalator travelling upwards. He looked down again and saw that she'd moved her feet further apart, now nearly shoulder-width. In the little mirror, he could see everything, and now noticed how thin the material of her white skirt was. It was almost paper-like, and it allowed lots of light in. As his excitement increased, the end of the escalator drew near. With trembling fingers he pushed the wire down and covered the mirror. The woman removed her hairband and shook her head, her hair tumbling over her shoulders and back. Then they stepped off, and she was gone.

Dalzon stood against the wall in the same spot as before, away from the flow of people. He closed his eyes, blocked out the surrounding noise and ran a mental replay. When he opened his eyes again he realised he was smiling, but the smile quickly faded. He reflected bitterly on the transitory nature of true happiness.

That night he dreamt of her. She was walking toward him in slow motion, her hair untethered and floating in all directions, as if blown by a gentle wind. Instead of a skirt and jacket she was wearing something like a white sheet, wrapped around her so that all her limbs were exposed to varying degrees. Her lips were blood-red, and she was smiling at him. Her smooth, fair arms rose and fell gracefully, her hips swayed from side to side. Dalzon reached out to her, but soon realised something; she wasn't getting any closer. He looked down and saw she was walking on a conveyor belt which was moving backwards. He tried to step onto it but became paralysed, trapped in an invisible force field preventing him from getting on. When he woke up the pain and frustration were still there, and his throat felt sore, as if he had been crying out. Dawn still hadn't broken. He lay awake for nearly an hour before dozing off into a turgid, dreamless sleep.

In the morning, feeling less than refreshed, he forsook the suit in favour of a pair of khaki chinos, a blue shirt and a brown pullover. He left his room at half past seven in the morning, knowing the journey from South to Central London would get him to Tottenham Court Road station at eight o'clock, just as it was getting busy. He managed to slipstream through the barriers at Kennington on the first attempt. When he reached his destination, took his usual position at the top of the escalator. This time however, he was looking not for new targets, but for her.

After half an hour of waiting, he gave up and went back to riding the escalators. Over the course of forty minutes he saw five gussets (one of them above a pair of hold-up stockings) a tattoo of a bear, and several varicose veins. Throughout it all he felt not a hint of nervousness; the previous day's apprehension and anticipation had turned into despondency. At ten o'clock he called it a day and returned home to his little room, feeling no better than he had when waking up from the dream.

Wednesday went pretty much the same way. He went earlier and spent nearly three hours in the station, but still there was no sign of her. Nothing made up for her absence – not one of the seven gussets, or even the pair of testicles he saw beneath one dress. He felt like a subterranean Sisyphus, growing wearier with each ascent.

The following day he managed to get a good view of a woman with no underwear. A brunette, she was tall, lean and wore a green dress with matching flat green shoes. It came as a surprise, as she didn't look the type not to wear knickers. It went to show, he reflected, that it really was unwise to judge people at face value. She'd drawn her feet closer together halfway along, blocking the view, but he didn't really care. He wondered why he was so unmoved, and questioned whether he was actually losing his capacity to feel anything. There was nothing wrong with her – she was probably in her late twenties, with good skin and quite shapely, slim legs. This was supposedly why he was doing what he was doing, going to all this trouble. If it no longer did anything for him, there was simply no point. A little later, as he gazed dispiritedly into his shoe mirror at the milky haunches of a stocky red-haired woman in her early forties, he began to suspect that he might be depressed.

The following day he returned for little reason other than it had become his routine, and a routine appealed to him a good deal more than sitting at home, which was more depressing than anything. He tried to look at the upsides. Firstly, he was getting good at what he was doing. He'd become adept at travelling for free, and he was proud of his design, the wire-controlled flap, which hadn't once failed him. He'd not been given one dirty stare in the last three days. Secondly, new plans were beginning to seed in his head. Hours of pretending to read the *Financial Times* had resulted in him actually absorbing some of the content. He didn't understand a great deal, but still he was starting to think about investments. The more he thought of his dingy little room, the more pervasive the thoughts were. He had to do something. When right at the bottom, he reflected as he looked up at the stream of sour-faced, descending commuters, there was only one way to go. He didn't have a lot of money, but his old employer had given him a lump sum redundancy payment, which he'd put aside. Since then he'd subsisted almost entirely on government benefits, managing to avoid dipping into the savings altogether. Perhaps it was time to dip in after all.

The next day, Saturday, was the hottest yet. He

dressed down further, donning a pair of faded, usefully roomy jeans and a white t-shirt with *Lomax Computing* written across the front. Likewise, when he arrived at the station he saw that very few in the crowd were dressed formally. Dalzon had become highly tuned to his environment. He noticed that each day had its own characteristics. The Monday throng was a little less dense, probably the result of staff calling in sick. Wednesday was the busiest, the faces less depressed than on the previous two days, despite being marooned in the middle of the week. Perhaps the trauma of transitioning from the weekend back to desk life had worn off by then.

Dalzon knew Saturday's crowd consisted mostly of shoppers, so he arrived at eleven, by which time it was really busy. The bulging carrier bags all around him were both a help and a hindrance. They provided extra shielding for his activity, but just as often they were placed between feet, rendering his mirrored foot useless.

At the top of his third ascent, he saw her. She was coming through the ticket barriers, wearing nearly exactly the same as she had on Monday; chunky heels, an above-the-knee white skirt and a formal charcoal jacket with a pinched waist. Her hair was down, covering her shoulders. She was walking slowly, looking not ahead but at the mobile phone in her hand. She wasn't carrying any shopping.

Glad he'd made a habit of buying the newspaper, he tucked it beneath his arm and performed exactly the same manoeuvre as before. He stood looking at his watch as if undecided about something then as she walked past, closed in behind her. He shivered with pleasure as he smelt her perfume, already so strong in its associations. He wondered what it was, where he could get hold of it, so that he might always relive this experience through smell. As she stepped onto the escalator she tied her hair up, exposing her neck. At the same time she widened her stance. At once Dalzon pulled up the flap and slid his foot forward between her meaty calves. It seemed that with her hair up, her scent was even stronger. He felt light-headed with pleasure.

Now he looked not only at the mirror but at the nape of her neck, her arms, her hair, the whole package. Her right hand clutched the strap of a small black leather handbag. He began to wonder what was inside it, and then heard a voice murmuring close to him. He turned around to see a tall youth wearing a red baseball cap and enormous pair of headphones gazing absently in front of him, above Dalzon's head. He heard it again, a voice close to him, saying something he couldn't make out. The lips of the boy behind him weren't moving. He span round again and looked at the back of her head, but the voice couldn't have been hers either; it wasn't coming from the right direction. They reached the foot of the escalator, and walking in the stiff style he'd perfected from necessity, Dalzon followed her all the way to the westbound train platform, where a train was arriving. Not wanting to be too obvious, he dropped back to let another commuter between them as the train slowed to a halt. A bright gleam hit his eye from below, and to his horror he realised he'd forgotten to lower the flap; the mirror on his shoe was reflecting the harsh, bright striplight above the platform into his eyes. He thrust his hand into his pocket, found the end of the wire and pushed it down. The flap slotted into place, and at the same time, the sliding doors banged shut. Dalzon watched the train pull away, the woman in the white skirt inside it. Almost out of view, she turned to face him and for a moment their eyes met.

He was numb, but as he made his way home, he began to feel comforted. Later that night, lying in his single bed and staring at the cracked ceiling and naked, forty-watt light bulb hanging from it, he felt something like a warmth inside, nurtured by the conviction that he would see her again. He felt untroubled by the shouts of the drunks outside, the noise of sirens, and even the groaning, clattering and bumping against and beyond the walls of his room.

Luckily for Dalzon, he had the time to spare.

He reasoned that if he continued the pattern of going early on weekdays and later on weekends, then provided her life was subject to any kind of routine, they were bound to meet again. Meanwhile, he was learning all the time. By gazing at the numbers in the newspaper each day, even without paying conscious attention, he began to notice certain trends – the slow but steady increase in value of cobalt and lithium Exchange Trade Funds, the relative steadiness and predictability of the gold market, the wild fluctuations in certain energy markets. He made a decision; he'd break into his savings and, one way or another, make a return.

On Tuesday morning she showed up, this time wearing knee-length boots and a short black dress. Once again, the moment he stepped on behind her she tied her hair up, exposing her neck and letting her perfume reach his nostrils unhindered. It was a decent enough view, but the thin, white material had worked so much better. Like a paper lampshade it had allowed the light through, whereas the black dress had the opposite effect. He withdrew his foot a little and in response, she inched back towards him, moving her feet farther apart as she did so. His heart beating hard, he wanted to say something to her, to tell her this dress wasn't working. As they neared the bottom, he heard the voice again.

"Shingasinga legrig," it said. Again he turned

around, this time to see a schoolgirl chewing gum. She stared insolently back at him, still chewing, and as he faced forward again he heard the pop of the gum-bubble she had just blown. He reached behind his head to make sure none of it had gone in his hair.

"Dreewee downder," said the voice, loud and yet a whisper at the same time. He wondered again if it was possible it was the woman in front of him. He angled his head and leaned forward, so that his ear brushed her pony tail, but he heard nothing more, and they reached the bottom. In one seamless movement she pulled off the hairband and shook her head, her hair tumbling over her shoulders. She walked off quickly this time, leaving him with the bizarre feeling of wanting to apologise to her.

The following day Dalzon waited two hours in vain without making a single trip down the escalator until he returned home. He wondered if he'd blown it with her.

On Wednesday, the day when the commuters seemed to cheer up, he found his usual spot near the top of the escalator occupied by a busker playing Beatles songs on a loud, jangly electric guitar hooked up to a small amplifier hanging from his belt. With his head thrown back and eyes closed as he sang, he was completely oblivious to the dirty stare Dalzon gave him. Given little choice, he decamped to the opposite side. It was an inconvenience; upon seeing her he would have to push his way through the stream of people coming off the upwards escalator in quick enough time to fall behind her. Even so it was the best remaining option. Standing anywhere else, he would have looked out of place and drawn attention to himself.

He'd grown so used to the station and its usual sounds, the hubbub of voices, the whirr of the escalators and the announcements from the overhead speakers, that he found the busker's presence thoroughly disruptive. He didn't even pause between his wretched songs. As Dalzon contemplated trying to get him moved or ejected by complaining to station staff, he saw her come through the ticket barrier, the same one she always went through. He moved at once, murmuring apologies as he edged through the two-deep line of commuters leaving the escalator for the exit barriers, in the process treading on an elderly woman's foot.

"Do you mind?" she snapped as the elbow of a big man in a suit nudged him painfully in the back. He made it across just in time. As he stepped behind her, she tied up her hair. Feeling both elation and relief, Dalzon closed his eyes and let the scent waft up to him, stimulating and caressing his senses and his imagination.

When he opened his eyes he noticed that she had new earrings, larger, more elaborate ones. She was wearing a light blue woollen sweater, but the white skirt was back. The sweater went well with her blonde hair, he thought. He smiled and held the folded newspaper to one side, his hand primed on the steel wire in his pocket.

Then he heard it again.

"Yakayeega barber, teberwear, ten."

It was hard to hear the voice against the shrill sound of the busker's music, and to make things worse, the man behind him kept coughing loudly. This time rather than trying to work out the source of the voice, he closed his eyes to listen. The music stopped.

"Seventy-five percent uptick," said the voice, and then it became muffled, as if by a hand clamped over a mouth. He opened his eyes and noticed that, for the first time, she had put her feet together. Dalzon looked down, his eyes wide, and then the man behind him sneezed, spraying the back of his neck without a word of apology. He wanted to turn around and confront him for the disgusting act, but didn't want to risk another payload directly in the face.

As she strutted off the escalator and whipped off her hairband, his eyes remained fixed to her rear, causing him nearly to collide with a pushchair. He stood in a corner, his mind racing, the pestilential chorus once again assaulting his ears from the upper level. For the rest of the day he remained so lost in his thoughts that he forgot to eat.

On Thursday the busker was gone and Dalzon was able to resume his usual spot. He wondered how much he'd made. There had certainly been lots of coins in his guitar case. He probably made more murdering popular songs for a few hours than Dalzon got every fortnight from the government.

This time as she came from the ticket barrier to the escalator, she caught his eye. Completely unprepared, he looked down at once, and was so hesitant in following her that they were nearly separated by a couple holding hands. Having reassured himself that the pair behind him were preoccupied with each other, he opened his newspaper and lifted the flap on his shoe. At the same time she put up her hair, this time smoothing out her pony tail with her hands. For the first time, he noticed a ring on her wedding finger. As soon as he put his foot forward, he heard it again.

"Kensuzi Telecommunications, medium-term hold."

This time there was no mistaking it; the voice was coming from between her legs. He tried to tilt his ear downward to hear better.

"Temposuki metalworks, short-term hold, twenty-nine days. Shinto Plastics, medium to long-term hold, nineteen months."

He wondered if the couple behind could hear it too. He turned his head further, not far enough to see them, but enough to hear the slurps of their kissing. At the same time the voice in his other ear became muffled again. He looked down to see she'd put her feet together once more, and realised it was probably because he'd withdrawn his own foot. He lifted his hand to tap her on the shoulder, but then they reached the bottom, she unleashed her hair, and was gone. He didn't follow her. He stood beside an illuminated hand cream poster, opened his *Financial Times* and leafed through it until he reached the International Stock Markets section. There it was. Kensuzi Telecommunications, Shinto Plastics and Temposuki metalworks were all listed on the Tokyo Stock Exchange.

The following day was Friday, but Dalzon didn't dress down. He wore his green pinstripe and even polished his shoes, flap and all. She looked at him again as she passed. This time he held her gaze. Now he saw her face properly, he noticed that her eyes were a little sad. This time he took care not to withdraw his foot from between her calves. The moment he heard the voice, he tucked the newspaper under his left arm and took a pocketbook and pen from inside his suit.

"Sakurako Waste Disposal, hold five days."

He cursed silently as the pen dried up. The voice

stopped speaking. As she walked away, she turned around, looked at him again, and smiled. He smiled back and contemplated waving for a moment, then felt daft. He realised his throat was sore. He was coming down with something.

For the rest of the weekend he was confined to bed, getting out only to empty his bladder and vomit in the yellow-walled, creaking shared bathroom. It was bound to happen sooner or later, in close proximity with so many strangers with so many germs flying around. Although he couldn't be sure, it was most likely the man who had sneezed over him. He shuddered as he remembered the man's gargling, rasping coughs, fearing he was in for a hard time. He was proved right. It started with sniffing, blowing his nose constantly, then coughing. By Sunday it hurt to breathe. Every time he coughed, it felt as if his chest were being ripped out. He fantasised about booting the sniffing, hacking disease-giver down the full length of the Tottenham Court Road escalator. With nothing to keep him occupied but a little radio and some old novels, he spent another two days at home before venturing back out again. The first thing he did when he went out on Wednesday morning was buy a copy of the *Financial Times*, which he took to a greasy spoon café. As was his habit he leafed quickly through it, scanning through the articles first before looking at all the numbers.

Then he saw a headline which made tea spill from his lips onto the formica.

Following a surprise takeover by the giant Yukihito Service Corporation that morning, the price of shares in the beleaguered, written-off, junk-status Sakurako Waste Disposal had increased by a completely unprecedented 370 per cent. When the waitress came and asked him if he was okay he heard nothing, and only looked up when she touched him on the shoulder.

On Thursday he took six pens, a pencil and sharpener with him. She arrived at the usual time, this time with her hair already up, pleated at the sides in a fifties style. She was wearing his favourite skirt, or at least one very much like it, and a purple sweater with a low neckline and the sleeves pushed up past her elbows. With the newspaper under his arm, he wrote down everything he heard, barely looking into the mirror although he held his foot in place the whole time. At one point she drew her legs together so her calves squeezed his feet. By the time they reached the bottom, he had filled an entire page of the notebook.

On Friday, for the first time, he left the mirror mechanism at home. It was a sweltering summer day and, being dress-down day for many workers across London, he knew he wouldn't draw too much attention. The breeze felt good around his toes and his legs. Wearing shorts felt nothing short of liberating, and the slowing of his walking pace from wearing flip flops was still nowhere near as restricting as a stiff wire down his trousers. He felt positively dynamic. When they met at the top of the escalator, he detected something like disappointment in her expression. She looked him up and down, then he was behind her again. Although no longer wearing the mirrored shoe, he slid his foot between her calves. He didn't want her putting her feet together again. His pen was readied, but he heard nothing. Halfway down the escalator stopped abruptly, throwing him forward into her. As he mumbled apologies she turned around, saw the pen and pad, and gently took them from his hands. Dalzon felt like voiding his bowels as she turned her back on him. He quivered as he thought of her leafing through the previous pages. Perhaps she wanted to punish him for having the audacity to turn up in shorts and flip flops, without the mirror. Maybe he deserved whatever was coming to him.

She turned around and smiling her slightly toothy smile, handed the pen and pad back to him. There was a telephone number in the middle of the page and beneath it, a name: Elaine. They reached the bottom and off she went, her hips swaying noticeably more than usual.

Dalzon didn't return for several weeks, but he kept

the number. When he eventually called, her voice was far softer than he'd imagined it would be. He realised as she spoke that he could no longer picture her face at all. Her ankles, legs, hips, the back of her neck, even her ears, he could visualise as if they were still right in front of him. He could even summon her smell in his memory, as well as the sensation of her tied-up hair brushing his mouth and nose. But the face was gone.

They met on a wednesday evening in a Sushi restaurant. She wore a black dress, her hair down, her lips a striking red. Dalzon was wearing a suit. Not the old green suit, but a new, fitted one made from Gabardine wool. It was the first time he'd worn clothing which fitted properly and it still felt strange to him, as did the Italian leather shoes on his feet. He had the feeling he was wearing somebody else's clothes.

"You look nice," she said. "Different, but in a good way. Really smart. It suits you."

He nodded and murmured in appreciation as he picked up the menu. It all looked the same to him, both the names and the pictures, and besides, he was too distracted to make a decision. All the dishes looked to him like female pudendae. Finally he decided to copy her set option choice of miso soup followed by salmon sashimi.

He watched her stir wasabi into a pool of soy

sauce with her chopsticks, then carefully followed her example. They ate in silence for a while, during which he again noticed the ring on her wedding finger. She saw him staring at it, then put down her chopsticks and covered it with her other hand.

"It's not how you think. He barely speaks to me. I can't remember the last time he asked me how my day was. He won't be home tonight, or the next two nights. It's this work, it takes him away all the time. He's never around."

Dalzon's eyes watered and he winced. He had put far too much wasabi on his sashimi. He let out a spluttering cough, and she pulled out a tissue and leaned over.

"Are you alright? Here, take this. Shall I ask the waiter for some water?"

He shook his head, waved his hand and sipped wine to quell the sting.

"There's something about you. You're sweet." She began to eat again.

"People think I should be happy because I live in a nice, big house, and I could choose not to work if I felt like it. But they don't understand. Nobody does. It's like I'm existing, not living. I feel like I have no purpose. What about you?"

Dalzon coughed again. All he could think about was coming up with a pretext to get beneath the table.

"All those times we went down that escalator together, then I'd get my train, but you never got on with me. Where did you go? Where do you go?"

A waiter approached. "Is everything okay? Are you enjoying the food?"

"Very much, thank you," she said with a brief smile. She was definitely more attractive when she didn't smile, he thought.

"Well, it's probably better I don't know," she continued. "It's not like I want to to tell you about my life. Not just you, anyone. I mean, there is nothing to talk about. That's really the truth."

"Mmmm-hmm."

Rrruuff!

They watched as a small, rust-coloured basset hound trotted down the aisle beside them. It stopped near the counter, panting, then came over to their table. It sniffed Dalzon's ankle, poked its nose up through the tablecloth and between his legs, then withdrew beneath the table again. Seizing the opportunity, Dalzon lifted the tablecloth and looked under. The basset looked back at him, tongue out, then licked his hand. He bent down lower, pulled a pen from his inside pocket and shooed the dog away.

"Oh, that dog is adorable. But what's he doing in a restaurant?" he heard her say.

Finally the dog turned, wagged its tail in his face,

and pushed its way back out again.

"Are you alright?"

He was listening for something else. Still beneath the table, the tablecloth draped over his back, he was straining with his ear poised between her knees, scribbling on the back of his hand. He noticed she was wearing shoes he hadn't seen before; black heels with gems embedded in the toes.

He saw the waiter's shiny shoes glide by, and extricated his head from beneath the table. She had stopped eating and was looking at him with a mournful expression. An argument was beginning at a nearby table.

"I'm sorry, madam," said the waiter. "Dogs are not allowed in this restaurant."

"Why didn't you say anything when we came in? We've ordered now."

"I'm sorry, but it's strict policy. Animals are not allowed in here, unless it's a…"

"Bring me the manager."

"I am the manager. I'm sorry madam. The dog has to leave."

With considerable noise, clattering and ceremonious scraping of chairs, the couple got up and left, the dog following them.

"Do you find me boring?"

He shook his head, coughed, and a chopstick fell to the floor. "Hold on," she said, looking around.

"I'll get him to bring some more."

But Dalzon was already under the table again. The chopstick was nestling between her feet, but he ignored it and whipped out the pen for the second time.

"Hey, it's okay, he's going to bring a new one," he heard her say.

He noticed she was moving her feet apart. Her hands appeared, gripped the sides of her skirt, and hoisted the hem up several inches. He heard the sounds of glassware being moved above him, then the thud of the wine bottle as she placed it back on the table. Then he saw the waiter's shoes again, inches from his face, pointing towards him. Once more he resurfaced.

"Here you go." She held out the fresh chopsticks in their paper sheath. As he took them she touched the back of his hand, which was festooned with numbers written in blue ink. "What's that?"

He pulled his hand back. "Nothing, just... reminders."

"I'm sorry. I suppose I don't have the right to ask you about what's on your hand any more than you do about what's on mine."

She took a long sip from her wine-glass.

"I think he's having an affair too," she said. "God, why am I even saying think? I know it."

She poked at her food with the chopsticks, moving

pieces around the plate.

"You don't like me, do you?"

Dalzon coughed again, deliberately this time. He stooped over in his chair and, pulling a face, pretended to fiddle with his shoe, as if something was stuck inside. As he drifted slowly downwards, she reached over and grabbed his arm.

"Wait," she said. "I get it. Look, I don't judge you for wanting that. You're only a man. But please, can we just talk? You'll have as much of it as you want, later. I promise."

He slowly straightened up again, and as the waiter caught his eye, he signalled for the bill. As they waited he gingerly placed his ink-free hand over hers and stroked it as comfortingly as he could. She smiled at him, but her eyes remained sad.

That night as she slept curled around him in his single bed, her bare form gently rising and falling, he reflected. Nothing was immune to change. He'd started off looking for one thing, and in finding it, found something else that he wanted more. It was ironic that one's aims, once achieved, changed fundamentally in nature. It wasn't so long ago that the mere thought of glimpsing in his shoe mirror what was now right beside him, exposed in the penumbra, had him losing sleep with excitement. But it hadn't been long before he'd lost interest in seeing it or touching it, and become interested only in listening to it. And he'd listened all night, as she slept, and taken notes until he himself had fallen asleep. Now he could think only of his new ambitions. He pictured himself standing on a balcony high up in a prestigious part of the city, a concierge calling up to confirm his taxi had arrived to take him wherever he wished to go. She turned her head, let out a rasping snore, and like a bubble pricked with a pin, the picture evaporated.

He pushed her away in irritation. There were no absolute truths. Life did not have to be a struggle and happiness did not, after all, have to be fleeting. He reached over, across the notepad covered with fresh numbers and writing, and turned off the bedside lamp. He drifted into dreams of faraway lands with emerald seas and golden sands, beneath bright blue skies. When he woke in the morning, she was gone. In a momentary panic he looked across to the bedside table; the notepad was still there. Reading directly from the pad, he called his broker and instructed him. This time, everything was to be invested. Every penny.

Autumn passed quickly, and the golden leaves which crunched underfoot were soon replaced by dark brown husks and slush. The days shortened and darkened, and pubs became cosier, their crackling fires offering warm relief from the bitter cold outside, but still Elaine did not return his calls.

Every week, he called his broker. The news was never encouraging, but he held out hope that the tide would turn. It had to.

One particularly cold, unforgiving evening, Dalzon took a walk. Harsh rain pricked at his skin like pin-points, and the wind blew hard. He stood on the pavement for a while. He felt his breathing was restricted, and his stomach ached as if he had been winded. Indeed, he wondered if being punched in the stomach by a professional boxer felt any different at all to losing everything one had. He moved closer to the road and stared into the traffic, fighting to keep his composure. As he watched the vehicles go by, he began to compare them and wonder what would take him out most efficiently; a double-decker bus or an HGV. It would depend on the speed, of course. If he was going to do it, he didn't want the job half-done. The wind and rain spat at him, and he drew his cashmere scarf tighter around his neck.

With his hands in his pockets, his collar up and head down, he forged through Russell Square, past the restaurants and hotels of Bloomsbury, past beggars, addicts, shoppers and drinking students, eventually arriving at Tottenham Court Road underground station. He scanned the ticket hall for station staff, and then, deploying a move he'd used too many times to forget, slipped through the entry barriers behind an elderly man.

He felt a range of emotions as he stepped onto the moving stairway. The anger had mostly subsided. It was hard to be angry when you'd lost everything, although when he got the bad news he'd first accused his broker playing a joke on him, then of making a mistake. It wasn't anger as much as blind panic at his own impotence and utter helplessness in the face of reality, a reality which yelling at his broker would not change. Then he thought about her. It seemed silly to blame her for something over which she had ostensibly no control or influence. The truth was he'd known she was hurt even as they'd dined in the restaurant. The fact she'd chosen to spend the night with him didn't change that. But it changed everything else.

As he was carried down the escalator he almost imagined he could feel the cold, hard steel wire running down his right leg. Although many months had gone by, he recognised many of the faces. None of them, of course, recognised him. They all remained wrapped up in their newspapers, their mobile phones, their lives. As he neared the bottom he heard a train rumbling in. A bus or a lorry might fail to do the job, he thought, but the tube wouldn't; That roaring hundred-ton mass of metal, machinery and human cargo would take care of everything, forever. Afraid of his own thoughts, he turned and stepped onto the upwards escalator. Then he saw her.

She coming down, wearing a black formal jacket over a white shirt. He thought about calling out, then saw the man behind her. Despite the opened newspaper in his hands he was looking directly down. It was clear she was standing as far back as she could on the moving step, her back pressed against him. Her eyes were closed, a faint smile on her lips.

Zaiko's Game

The steel door banged open, illuminating the cell with fluorescent light from the corridor outside. Tal, the younger prisoner, lay facing the wall. The other, Bane, looked up at the guard with swollen and bloodshot eyes. The guard spoke in a stilted manner.

"You've been given every chance to save yourselves, but refused to co-operate. Do you have anything to say before the death sentence is passed?"

Bane shook his head. The guard looked at the other prisoner, who appeared to be asleep, but Bane knew he was awake and listening.

"Then you'll both be executed in the morning," said the guard in his monotone. "But another choice remains open to you. One of you can walk free tomorrow."

The striplights behind the guard flickered for several seconds.

"I will return at nine o'clock in the morning with a doctor. If the doctor certifies one of you is dead, the other will live and walk free. Who dies and who lives is entirely up to you."

The guard let the words hang in the air for some time.

"If you're both found alive, the two of you will be killed immediately. Do you understand?"

"Yes," said Bane with deliberation.

"The General is merciful. He has ordered you be brought anything you ask before then, except weapons or communication devices."

The guard turned on his heel and slammed the door behind him, plunging the cell once more into semi-darkness.

Tal turned and stared at Bane in the dim light.

"Was that a joke?"

"I'm afraid not. Zaiko is well known for these things."

Bane heard Tal's breathing quicken.

"I do feel for that guard. Imagine having to deliver those lines with a straight face," said Bane, trying to soothe the younger man with humour.

"What are we going to do?" said Tal in a cracking voice.

"Let me think."

For some time they sat in silence, facing each other on the wooden bunks. Bane felt Tal's terror, palpable in the air.

"What if we just talk?"

They normally took care to speak quietly, almost in whispers, but these words erupted as if Tal had suppressed them for some time.

Bane fixed him with a stare. He moved over to sit beside Tal, adjusting his position several times before leaning back against the wall. In addition to the cameras, four microphones were hidden in the cell. Bane knew where every one of them was. Keeping a shoulder blade firm against the tiles between which the closest microphone was embedded, Bane spoke in a low, quiet voice.

"Do you understand what will happen if they hear you saying that? If they think we're close to breaking? They'll torture us a thousand times worse than before. Until we die."

Tal's eyes were glazed with fear, but the older man knew how important it was to make himself understood.

"And you know what will happen if we do talk?"

Tal remained silent.

"They'll kill us immediately afterwards. We won't even live until dawn. We just die sooner, and we die as traitors."

"Then what are we going to do?" whispered Tal in a trembling voice.

"Just let me think for a while."

Bane tried to strip his thoughts of emotion, focusing on the thin orange filament inside the tiny bulb above. From the corner of his eye he saw Tal twitch. At once he saw his cellmate staring at him in a very particular way. It was a look Bane knew too well. He had seen it up close on men's faces, against them in combat. He silently forgave him, but decided it would be wise not to turn his back towards his fellow prisoner for one moment.

He got up and pressed the button by the door, eyes on Tal the whole time.

"What are you doing?" hissed Tal.

"Don't say anything," said Bane. "Not a word. Just let me do the talking."

They sat still as the guard's footsteps echoed down the corridor, growing gradually louder.

Less than one hundred metres above them, General Zaiko was busy in his pleasure palace. He had Esmerelda, his favourite concubine, kneeling on an Ottoman as he thrust into her from behind. His breathing grew shallower and harder. A string of saliva escaped the corner of his mouth, swinging loosely before pooling in the small of Esmerelda's back. Some of the other girls watched, reclining on chaise-longues and the variously sized beds lining the outer walls of the chamber. Close by stood the eunuchs, holding dishes of food, glasses of champagne and bowls of pharmaceutical drugs.

The General released a languid grunt as he climaxed despite himself. Irritated, he rose up, shuffled backward and flopped onto a chaise-longue. Esmerelda slowly rearranged herself and sat upright, drawing her knees together on the Ottoman. Zaiko looked at her for some time, muscles clenching in his cheeks.

"Fetch Astor," he said to Elman, the head eunuch. Elman wore a similar red robe to the other eunuchs, but with white trim. All the eunuchs' clothing was designed to match the furniture of the pleasure palace.

Astor, the strongest and most athletic of the eunuchs, was sleeping, having been on duty the previous twelve hours. Elman returned with him. Astor was slender, tall, shaven-headed like the other eunuchs but with uniquely striking features. He had high, sharply defined cheekbones and preternaturally smooth skin, in some ways resembling a magnificent porcelain doll.

"Your eminence," said Astor.

The General pointed to Esmerelda. "Use your tongue. Don't stop until she is satisfied."

Astor stood still as if processing the instructions, then bowed his head, went to Esmerelda and knelt before her. Her knees slowly parted as she pulled up her silk gown. Within minutes her demeanour switched again. No longer did she seem shy and self-conscious, there in the middle of the pleasure palace, surrounded by the attendants and the other girls. Her eyes closed and her mouth opened as Astor went to work. She rested a hand on his large, bald head, which undulated softly between her legs like a buoy in a calm sea.

The General watched with intense focus. Esmerelda's hips moved almost imperceptibly at first, then thrust back and forth with increasingly violent movements. Clutching Astor's head with both hands, she pulled him in hard. At length she let out a long moan.

The General summoned a eunuch with a tray, reached inside one of the bowls, lifted a pinch of white powder to his nostrils and took a huge sniff.

All the other girls were watching now. Astor shifted as if readying himself to get up, but Esmerelda hadn't finished. She moaned deeper and louder, then gave a loud cry which echoed around the pleasure palace. Her scarlet nails dug into the back of Astor's skull.

The General twitched in his seat. Elman, standing close by, threw his master a nervous glance.

"That's enough," said Zaiko, but the General could barely be heard above Esmerelda's cries. Elman stepped towards the Ottoman then stood still as if unsure what to do next.

"Stop," roared the General, rising to his feet, his face purple with rage. Astor pivoted to one knee in an attempt to rise, but Esmerelda held him down with such force that even with all his strength, he struggled. A rivulet of blood ran down the back of his heavily scratched head.

"My lady," he breathed in desperation, but Esmerelda was in another realm. Her eyes rolled back in her head, her cries grew louder, and still she held his head tight. Finally Elman stepped forward and prised them apart. Astor fell back and his long body flopped across the floor. He gasped as if saved from drowning. The chief eunuch helped him to his feet.

"Well, that was entertaining," said Zaiko cheerfully. "Now put him to death."

"Your eminence, please," said the chief eunuch.

"You want to defy me?" said Zaiko.

"Your eminence, show mercy. He didn't intend wrong."

"Do you want to live?" said Zaiko, addressing Astor directly.

"Yes, your eminence," said Astor.

The General moved close to Astor and studied him from head to foot with narrowed eyes.

"He wants to live," said Zaiko seemingly to himself. He looked across to Esmerelda, who had apparently regained awareness.

"He wants to live," repeated the General to his favourite.

"Spare him," said Esmerelda, her palms pressed together.

"You hear that? She wants you spared," said General Zaiko to Astor. "But let's be honest, she would say that, wouldn't she!"

The General shrieked with laughter. Esmerelda bowed her head.

"Alright, alright. Let him live," the General said, waving a hand.

"Your eminence," said Elman, lowering his head.

"But remove his tongue."

Astor cried out as he was hauled away by two guards. He didn't resist, but his feet dragged across the floor as he was removed from the pleasure palace.

Back deep below a guard left cell 215, slamming the heavy door behind him. Tal and Bane looked at what the guard had left behind on the cell floor; a black plastic box and on top of it, a gold coin and a digital wristwatch. Bane picked up the watch and studied it.

"We can't do this," breathed Tal. "We can't. We can't do this."

"You know the options," said Bane in a calm and clear tone, putting the watch round his wrist. "One of us dies, or we both die."

He picked up the coin and turned it around in his fingers. "This is the only fair way to do it."

From afar came sounds of creaking, slamming and murmuring.

"Do you want to flip it, or shall I?"

"Let me do it." said Tal.

"As you wish."

Bane sat back as Tal took the coin with trembling hands. He made the sign of the cross, closed his eyes, then flipped it up into the air. The sound of the coin hitting the concrete floor, spinning for a moment then settling seemed deafening. Slowly Tal opened his eyes. Seeing the result, his head sank into his hands.

"What now?" said Tal.

"We still have time," said Bane, looking at the watch. "So we wait."

And the two men waited. Neither fell asleep, but Tal's head dipped time and time again. Just as his chin touched his chest, he would abruptly sit up straight again before repeating the cycle. Bane sat still with his back against the wall, feet up on the bunk. Every now and then he glanced at the watch. Save for the occasional sound of distant doors closing and the even fainter murmur of voices, they were shrouded in silence.

"It's time," said Bane finally. "Are you ready?"

The younger man nodded. They stood up together.

"When?" said Tal.

Bane looked at the watch, then put his ear to the cell door. In the distance he heard several voices, footsteps, a heavy door opening and closing. He knew it was the first cell in the row, down the far end of the corridor. They were checking them one by one. He closed his eyes as if calculating something.

"Now."

Tal turned his back to Bane, then once again made the sign of the cross. Bane wrapped an arm round the younger man's neck and firmly pulled tight. Tal's whole body tensed, relaxed, tensed again, then struggled. Tal's fingers now prised at Bane's arm, but he applied more pressure still. Tal's weight pulled Bane's arm downward as his legs gave way. He held tighter still, until Tal stopped moving. The noises from outside were much louder now. They were two cells away. Bane released his cellmate, and he fell motionless to the ground. It was nine o'clock.

The cell door opened, and the guard entered with the doctor. Another two guards remained outside.

"Stand back," said the guard. Bane moved away as the doctor knelt down beside Tal. He felt his wrist, his throat, then ripped open his shirt and put a stethoscope against his chest for what seemed a very long time.

Finally the doctor looked up at the guard and nodded.

"Do you wish for a priest?" said the guard. "No," said Bane immediately. There were many things he could have said to the guard, many things he could have asked him over time, but somehow he felt it unnecessary, even pointless. Over the course of all the small interactions, the hundreds of checks, cell visits, the scripted lines he was ordered to read to the prisoners, Bane had carefully observed the man assigned to watch them. Behind the unchanging expression which seemed to give so little away, Bane nevertheless saw the eyes were not those of a tyrant, nor of a bully.

"I'm sorry for your loss," said the guard. Bane nodded in acknowledgement, then flipped the black case open. He removed the lubricated defibrillator pads, placed them on Tal's bared chest and activated the current. Tal's body jolted violently. Bane looked up at the guard, even as he pressed the trigger repeatedly. The guard watched in silence.

Tal's body shuddered each time only to immediately fall limp again. Without taking his eyes off the guard, Bane pressed again and again.

On the fourteenth attempt, Tal twitched violently and made a retching sound.

Bane was fully prepared to be shot on the spot. And yet somehow he knew that the man standing over him would simply carry out his orders to the letter. No less. And no more. The guard dismissed the doctor from the cell.

"I must report to his eminence," said the guard. Bane slowly nodded as he held Tal's head in his arms.

The younger prisoner released several loud, rasping breaths, his arms now flailing weakly.

General Zaiko sank back into the huge leather chair in the main study. He stretched out an arm before him, opening and closing his fingers. He grunted in frustration. His hand was cramping from hours of signing death warrants, and it was getting difficult even to write his own name. The papers lay in two piles on the mahogany desk; unsigned and signed. The pile of unsigned warrants was still the larger one, despite the progress made.

Close by stood Hanso, the General's secretary and chief administrator. Across the study, reclining under the large bay window was Esmerelda, playing on a mobile phone.

"Tell me something," said Zaiko. "Why do I have to sit signing these day after day like an idiot?"

"Your eminence, they require your authorisation," replied Hanso.

"But why can't I just tick them off instead of signing them? My hand is killing me."

"For proof of your authorisation, your eminence. To prevent mistakes or forgeries."

"So isn't there an easier way? Like a seal. I want a seal!" cried the General. "A signet ring to make wax seals. Like in mediaeval times."

Hanso coughed.

"At the very least a stamp. There you go, a stamp.

It's obvious really, if you think about it. So why didn't you?"

"We'll have one made, your eminence."

"What use are you to me, when it comes down to it?"

A guard approached and spoke quietly to Hanso.

"He's here," said Hanso. "Do you want to see him now?"

"Of course," said Zaiko. "Bring him in."

Bane was escorted in, a guard either side of him.

"I'm done with this for today," said Zaiko pointing at the piles of documents on the desk. "Take it away, and bring a chair for my guest."

Hanso summoned an assistant, and together they cleared the desk and left the study chamber.

"Please, sit down," said the General, studying Bane closely.

"Have my men mistreated you?"

"No," said Bane, thinking of the head guard, who he was fairly sure had a wife and children.

"Simply looking at you tells me you're not being honest. But I'll believe you. I like to think those working for me are more than common thugs."

Bane stared at the General in silence.

"Don't be afraid to speak. Don't you have any questions?"

"Where's Tal?" said Bane immediately.

"Your compatriot? We freed him."

"Freed him?"

"Yes, freed him. He was driven two hundred kilometres from here and released with a bag of provisions. I'm told he was in good physical health."

"Why should I believe you?"

"I'm sure you'll see the proof soon enough." The General leaned back in the leather chair. "That was very clever, what you did back there. With the defibrillator. How did you come up with that?"

"You don't know it was my idea."

"Of course it was," said the General. "Who could have pulled that off, other than he who came up with it? Can't have been much margin for error. Were you a doctor?"

"No."

"All the more impressive. You solved my little challenge, and now your friend is not only alive, but free. You saved him. Still, we had no reason to keep him. He wasn't much use to us. You, on the other hand, are something different."

Zaiko stood up and waved around him. "What do you think of my library?" He walked across the large room. "This section is devoted to the ancients. I lose myself for days here. The wisdom of Aristotle. Cicero, Plutarch. That great chronicler, Thucydides. It's hard to explore these accounts of great civilisations by such great men, and not feel we've gone backwards. Wouldn't you agree?"

"Yes," said Bane.

"If you only knew how starved I am of intelligent conversation. What depresses me most is the lack of curiosity these days. You're very quiet."

"What should I say?"

"It's always the way. The wisest speak the least. The silent buddha is the ultimate embodiment of wisdom. I'm flattering you now, I know. But you impressed me. I truly didn't expect what you did."

General Zaiko continued walking around the study.

"I know what they say about me in the news. I'll be honest, it hurts me. They say I take inspiration from bad Hollywood movies, as if I have no culture, no originality at all. No mention of any of this," said Zaiko waving towards another wall of books. "This section is devoted to the East. You see these here?" He pointed to one shelf lined with particularly ornate books. "I personally commissioned them. Newly translated, hand-written volumes of the Thousand and One Nights. You know them well, probably?"

"Yes."

"Of course!" said the General with delight. "As if I needed to ask. I've read every single one. Go on, test me. I can tell you what happens in every volume."

"I'll take your word for it."

"I take inspiration from all over, but I do love these

stories," said the General. "And now you'll recognise that I have cast you in the role of Scheheradze. You know, people think I create these little tests out of pure sadism."

"Surely not," said Bane.

"Unbelievable, isn't it? But why bother explaining that I'm hunting for treasure? Nobody understands me. I'm looking for cream, so I try to create scenarios where cream rises to the top. It almost never does. You've been a pleasant surprise in that regard."

"I'm honoured."

"Men thrive under pressure, don't they? My aim is to coax out human ingenuity, creativity in its purest form. In turn, I like to think my little trials are themselves highly creative acts."

The General returned to his chair. "Tell me, as one cultured, intelligent man to another. What could I do better? I value your opinion."

"I don't think you want to hear it."

"Please, don't be so modest."

Esmerelda adjusted her position on the chaise-longue beneath the window, and both men looked over at her. She smiled at Bane. Bane had not seen a woman for years. In Esmerelda's beauty, her softness, her elegance, he saw not one woman, but all of womankind in one embodiment. In her he saw his own beloved wife.

"She's beautiful, isn't she?"

"Yes," said Bane.

"I think she likes you. Her name is Esmerelda. Say hello, my treasure!"

"Hello," purred the General's favourite, waving a hand softly.

"I can't promise I have others more beautiful than her. But they come close. I'm a man of taste."

"What do you want?" said Bane.

"Your answer, obviously. Will you do it?"

"Do what?"

"Work for me," said the General in apparent surprise. "What else?"

The silence hung in the air before Bane finally answered.

"I'd rather die."

The General rose to his feet. "This is disappointing. It took me so long to find you. And you did so well. Your friend is alive. You're alive. And I'm offering you the opportunity of a lifetime."

"Go to hell."

The General stared at Bane for some time. His expression changed, and his jaw muscles clenched. His chest rose and fell quickly.

"Have it your way," said Zaiko, removing the pistol from his side holster. "You might want to look away, my treasure," he shouted in Esmerelda's direction. He raised the barrel and pointed the gun directly between Bane's eyes. His hand was trembling. Bane stared into the General's eyes without blinking. Zaiko's hand trembled more still, and his jaw clenched furiously. He inhaled sharply and pressed the trigger. Esmerelda gave a sharp cry and jolted as the shot rang out, echoing around the library.

Several guards ran into the room, machine guns primed. General Zaiko stood looking down at Bane's body as the men slowly lowered their guns. "What the hell are you morons staring at?" shrieked the General. "Get out!" The guards slowly backed out of the library. Esmerelda sat upright, a look of horror on her face, eyes fixed on Zaiko.

The General fired the remaining shots into the wall and then hurled the pistol to the ground. He sat at his desk for several minutes, then in one violent movement, swept the ornate lamp, glass paperweight and marble inkpot from the desk, sending them crashing to the floor. He inhaled deeply, then roared out loud like a wounded animal. When his breathing had returned to normal, he pressed a button to summon his staff.

* * *

Did you enjoy this book? If so, please leave a review on Amazon - it means a lot!

About the Author

Born in London, I have also lived in Russia, Germany and Poland. In another life I was a freelance data analyst. For info and updates on my writing, sign up by email on my website, alistairmoore.com.

You can connect with me on:
- http://alistairmoore.com
- https://twitter.com/DrPapoose
- https://www.facebook.com/alistairmooreauthor

Subscribe to my newsletter:
- https://www.alistairmoore.com

Also by Alistair Moore

The Release (Candy Jar Books 2018)
Revenge is a dirty word, but what would you do if you met your child's killer?

Bennie goes largely unnoticed by those around him, something he has turned into a vocation. His world is upended when a violently bereaved father offers him a life-changing amount of cash for information about his son's murderer, soon to be released from prison.

Against a background of colourful characters, social division and brutalist inner-city architecture, Bennie finds himself caught up in another man's quest for vengeance, tested to the limit as he digs into the past of a boy who became a killer.

Ultimately Bennie is forced to confront questions of morality and justice, redemption and the true meaning of freedom.
Available from Amazon & all good bookshops.

Printed in Great Britain
by Amazon